James

Book 1 of The Patterson Brothers Series

L.B. Brookes

Contents

Dedication

i

To my family, for they make all things possible

Acknowledgments

Brian- as always, you are my hero in our story.

About the Author

L.B. Brookes writes contemporary romance novels that revolve around intrigue and danger. This danger brings everything to the surface. She likes sharing the excitement of her characters handling the emotions of falling in love while fighting for what is important to them. Good, bad, right or wrong gets thrown into the mix while her characters become better versions of themselves. Love truly matters.

When L.B. Brookes is not writing, she is sailing on the Chesapeake Bay with her husband, family, and friends. When that isn't possible, she enjoys all forms of artwork, reading a good book, doting on her cat, and enjoying her quiet times.

L.B. Brookes enjoys hearing from her readers, so please send her an email at lbb@lbbrookes.com

Chapter One

Despite the intense pain radiating throughout his body, he refused to succumb. He had endured worse before, but this was different. More concerning was the numbing coldness that wanted to engulf him. His 68W combat medic's knowledge warned him of the severity of these symptoms, but the elite special ops soldier remained resolute. He focused on staying upright, putting distance between himself and his present location, leaving those fallen enemies behind.

As the shitstorm neared its end, the soldier accepted that there should be no trace left of the ones who had come to rescue Lia Robinson. This, above all else, had to be enough.

However, the loss of what could have been hurt more than his physical wounds.

At least Lia is safe and on her way home, the soldier's silent relief expressed.

Now, the rest of the team could do what he, with regret, could not. They would be the ones to personally deliver Lia—safe and sound—to her family's doorstep.

And for him, not seeing Marshall's face when he found out about the significant rule broken on this mission would be regrettable, too. A rule that even this hardened soldier had thought impossible to break.

Letting emotions get the best of him wasn't something he customarily allowed. But taking a page from Marshall's playbook—"Go big or not at all"—certainly played a hand in what went down.

James Patterson had fallen hard for his commander's goddaughter.

A laugh burst from his lips, caused the pain to come back with a vengeance. The sudden agony made him stumble and drop to his knees, his hands scraping against the rocky shards that littered the ground.

It didn't matter that the impact of the unforgiven landscape jarred leg muscles, as well as the multiple injuries throughout his chest and side. It didn't matter that the bloody wounds soaked into the shirt and pants, staining the fabric a darker brown.

None of that mattered.

He still had to get further away from the small village. His proximity to the enemy's camp mattered more than his injuries.

His heated exhales met the approaching dusk's cooling air, forming puffs of mist before they faded away into nothingness.

James grunted and pushed onward, searching for a place to hide. A place to die, where they wouldn't recover his body.

If Mexico's leader knew of their interference—though warranted—it could jeopardize good relations. But what they didn't know couldn't hurt them.

No one had given chase for a couple of hours now. The few straggling hired guns who had been a problem after their initial escape were no longer a concern. But the next few days would likely be another story.

The remaining leaders of this network would have questions. They would bring an army to ravage these parts, seeking answers—or more likely, revenge. Even with the damage done by James and his team to this drug-smuggling operation, the cartel's setback wouldn't last long.

What? A few months? Maybe a little longer? James figured.

It wouldn't be more than a blip on anyone's radar before business was operational once more. Hopefully, by then, the reasons behind Lia's abduction would have answers—and resolutions.

Toppling again, James threw his weight toward a nearby tree. The jagged bark cut into his already shredded palms, but given his two equally inconvenient options, the lesser one won out. It became exceedingly difficult for him to remain upright. If he dropped again, getting back up might not be an option.

The tree's broad trunk supported his tall, battered frame. Sweat and grime blurred his vision, and wiping it away only made matters worse. A soft curse escaped his lips as the dirt and blood on his hands stung his eyes.

He shook his head, fighting the fog threatening to consume him. Dizziness hit him hard, and he gripped the trunk tighter, waiting for it to pass.

Only a few more miles. He promised himself and pushed off the tree.

A vehicle's revving—fast and approaching—halted his forward momentum. His stomach sank. That short-lived belief that he had more time before the cartel sent more men was crushed.

His ravaged body turned to face the oncoming vehicle. The weary soldier shifted his stance, preparing to fight. What happened today couldn't be traced back to his country.

More importantly, those monsters wouldn't get to Lia or his brothers.

I'll take a few more of you bastards to the grave with me.

A vehicle barreled along the uneven terrain, heading directly for him. With the last ounce of his remaining strength, he prepared to launch his power at the unwanted company.

A soft voice whispered in his head.

It's me...

James' reserves deflated as quickly as they had surfaced. A string of foul words left his mouth as his tired body sank to the ground. The battle to remain standing was forfeited.

She's supposed to be miles away from here.

That thought wanted to be yelled but he didn't possess the strength to do so—besides a part of him burst with happiness at seeing her.

One last time.

An old Chevy truck—more rust than red—swerved and skidded to a stop. Its forward motion halted just inches from the soldier's slumped frame, kicking up dirt and pebbles with its abrupt shift. The jungle, with its dense foliage and ominous silence, stood in stark contrast to the battered truck's running engine on the rocky path.

James heard the grating of metal scrape against metal as the door swung open. Then, the rapid pounding of hurried footsteps superseded a startled gasp. A pair of hands began pulling on his clothes and arms. A groaned complaint escaped from his mouth. He just wanted to rest.

"Move," she commanded. "Don't you dare lie down."

He struggled to comply. His head felt light, his thoughts hazy, while his body weighed heavy—like molten lead-filled bones wanting to solidify. Every movement felt as if he were battling against the weight of the world. His limbs seemed heavy and unresponsive. However, the persistent tugging gave him no choice but to follow where it pulled and prodded him along.

At this point, things quickly faded in and out of awareness. The sounds and images of the surrounding jungle became disjointed, like a bad connection on a video conference. Yet, despite his feeble attempts at coordinated mobility, progress must have happened because a sudden cold, unyielding, cantilevered surface jabbed James in the hip. Another set of hands, larger and stronger, dragged him up onto a horizontal ledge. A rigid object of ribbed metal pressed into his back.

That enveloping coldness seeped thoroughly into him, like a thousand icy needles piercing his skin. His teeth began rattling violently together. The shivering vibrations made his whole body scream in agony. The glaring brightness of distorted shapes started to darken and narrow into a tiny sphere until even this pinpoint grew dimmer and dimmer. Soft voices murmured above him, and then a singular voice whispered in his left ear.

Only her voice kept him tethered to that truck's flatbed.

"You won't die today, James. I'm planning on marrying you. We're gonna have two kids and a dog. Don't. You. Dare. Die on me." Her words were a lifeline, a beacon of hope in the darkness.

An airy lightness filled him—joy so intense he wondered if the brightness showed outwardly. He started to smile before everything faded into a dark, empty void.

Upon awareness the next time, James sorely missed that earlier coldness. Now, a fiery hell surrounded him—one where escape seemed as impossible as grasping a handful of smoke.

Already convinced that hell awaited him after death, his mind wandered. *I guess I didn't make it. Boy, will Lia be pissed at me.*

But another part of him thought it just might be for the best.

A balm of wetness and coolness touched his lips, soothing the heat momentarily. The liquid coated his parched lips and scratchy throat. Fearing it would disappear, he greedily drank.

That dread soon became a reality when the container against his mouth disappeared. His uncoordinated limbs fumbled and struggled, desperate to bring back that soothing moisture that had briefly relieved him.

"Relax," a low voice murmured. "Don't worry. There will be more. In a little bit." Fingers brushed across his chin, spreading the droplets of water along the contours of his face. This film of liquid got absorbed quickly into his hot, dry skin. "Go back to sleep," the voice said softly.

He knew this soothing voice. It was familiar to him. James wanted to stay awake to hear more of its musical cadence. At one time, he thought the voice's owner would be a penance—just one of many other opportunities needed to mete out justice to counter all the blemishes on his soul.

But this mission had quickly become personal. And she had become more—so much more—than just a penance. Lia had swiftly become the reason he'd risk it all.

The weighing fatigue swiftly overwhelmed him again. However, this time, his mind didn't escape into an empty void of nothingness.

This time, he dreamed of coming face-to-face with Lia Robinson—when everything he knew about himself drastically altered.

A half a world away, Frank Marshall did everything humanly possible to get them back home. Alive.

Frank's unwavering commitment to keeping lives safe for so many people was a duty he embraced without hesitation. Always. And hopefully, he'd continue this honor until the day he stopped breathing. But now, the stakes had been raised to a whole new level.

With his infinite resources, Frank needed to bring people—family—back home, all while avoiding an international incident between the United States and Mexico.

In the privacy of his home office, he could admit the truth. Avoiding an international incident was nonsense. A lie. He had no problem causing an incident if that was what it took to bring them home.

After all, wasn't I responsible? Franks' rationale posed. He had sent the Patterson brothers into that unsanctioned battlefield. The weight of that decision hung heavy on his shoulders.

After disconnecting from the recent phone call, Frank Marshall set the receiver back on the device's base and sank deeper into the chair. His head tilted against the headrest, and Frank stared unseeingly at the ceiling. As the memory surfaced, his thoughts were consumed by that singularly deliberate decision, which set this course of events into play.

James

Chapter Two

A week ago

Frank Marshall sat at a desk in his Annapolis residence's office.

An office adorned with dark walnut wood and layered in various shades of midnight blue reflected a perfect blend of style and effortless elegance.

The woman of the house, a woman of refined taste and a keen eye for design, reigned over all aspects of its décor, and this room was no exception. Yet, adoring her husband, she made sure the appearance considered his tastes as well.

Well, mostly.

She did help him out—adding just a few touches of whimsy.

Like the small frog-king lamp wearing a red cape that sat on the shelf alongside his military strategy books. Or the weathered sofa in dark leather that dominated the space, accompanied by two coordinating pillows. Seemingly conservative—until one flipped them over and read the funny quotes about enjoying life stitched in bold letters. These whimsical touches, amidst the serious décor, never failed to bring a smile to Frank's face.

His favorite was the glass-topped giraffe head and neck-shaped end table beside the red and blue checkered wingback chair placed by the window.

These minor enhancements—with deliberate calculation—suggested that lightness became possible even when things were at their darkest. Frank had dealt with darkness most of his professional adult life and needed this reminder many times over the years. Today, more than ever, these loving mementos helped keep the message viable, prompting a thoughtful reflection on the balance between these forces in Frank's life.

Frank looked up from the file on the desk upon hearing two sharp, consecutive knocks on his office door. While closing the thick-looking folder before him, he called out, "Come in."

The antiqued handle squeaked and turned. Frank watched the panel door as it swung open. His jaw clenched as he waited for his guest to cross the threshold. The man entering his private domain was James Patterson, a figure of authority and respect in Frank's professional life. Frank studied him with keen eyes, noting the signs of a seasoned warrior in his bearing and demeanor.

When James sat down, the chair creaked under his shifting weight. The guest chairs in this office needed to be substantial.

It was a good thing Jenna was familiar with the type of men her husband regularly worked with: big, tall, and all muscle.

Having known James for a decade—give or take—Frank couldn't help but compare that fresh-faced recruit he trained years ago with the seasoned soldier sitting before him today. The transformation was striking, a testament to the passage of time and the evolution of his character.

Just like Frank's younger self, James and the Patterson brothers excelled where few had ever done before. In some ways, James still crashed through obstacles unheedingly, which stumped many others, as if it were just a casual stroll through the park.

There lies the problem, Frank speculated. His shoulders shifted, and he settled back. A look went to the folder placed before him.

"Sir. You said it was urgent?" Like his brothers, James had that driving force that pushed one to go after the next-to-impossible mission.

His hands gripped and held tight to the sturdy wood frame. The eagerness to jump back into the fray flashed within James' eerily colored eyes. Their usual freezing, icy-blue intensity now reflected the heat of a burning molten fire.

A seasoned warrior couldn't sustain that intense focus without paying some steep price.

In some regards, death seemed the kinder fate, while the loss of one's self assured the harsher of the two outcomes. The darkness of all those assignments could seep into a man and not let go—a haunting reminder of the psychological toll of military service.

Frank recognized the telltale signs in the Patterson brothers because he, too, had faced the same difficulties at one time. If seasoned warriors didn't know how to counter their hardwired predator's nature, their souls would soon harden, just like their battle-worn bodies. *Too high of a price,* Frank surmised, *for honoring their country's duties.*

After all, Frank reasoned, *hadn't slamming right into Jenna alter mine?*

Jenna Marshall, the woman who had come and anchored—in a way no one on God's green earth could have managed—Frank's warrior spirit, was more than just a love interest. She was his wife, his partner in life and in battle. The love of this good woman had made it possible to lead this bone-weary warrior out of the darkness.

On instinct—whenever making difficult decisions like this—Frank's gaze went to his wife's framed photograph sitting strategically on the desk. That smile shined as bright as the day she came crashing into her husband's life.

The older man's expression turned determined. His attention locked onto James. "I have a job for you and your team." Frank slid the closed file across the surface between them and motioned for James to take it.

"Lia got abducted yesterday outside of San Juan Cotzocón. I believe someone falsely lured her there for the sole purpose of this abduction. They have since moved her to a small village within the Sierra Mixe district in the southwestern part of Mexico."

Frank knew it took an instinct to protect, partnered with years of training the mind and body, to make a great warrior.

The Patterson brothers were ready and willing to do what needed to happen, even if it meant they'd lay their lives down to save another.

Wasn't it usually for someone they didn't even know?

Frank's jaw clenched tight. This time, it proved different.

He was about to ask the team to save and protect someone they all knew—or more like it—knew of. Someone who wasn't just a mission, but a part of Frank's life.

As James opened the file, the photograph stapled to the inside cover immediately drew him in. He knew why keeping a distance from this particular woman had become a compelling habit over the recent years. Lia's picture could distract any man;

he proved no more immune than the rest. His conflicting feelings for her had become a constant battle.

Lia's caramel-colored brown, sparkling eyes hit James directly in the abdomen. The crinkles around her eyes and the upturned corners of her mouth showed affection toward whoever was taking her picture. Her tilted chin reflected her challenging nature, a trait that James found tempting.

But the laughing acceptance—caught forever on film—jerked his chain. Like it always did. This particular snapshot captured her trying to stop her golden blonde hair—cut to chin-length—from blowing in front of her face. Her pose and direct gaze into the camera reflected confidence and joy.

Lia enjoyed being outside and tanned easily. And like this shot, the other framed pictures throughout Marshall's home portrayed a warm skin tone that hinted at an apricot tint—like being perpetually kissed by the sun.

The humming of the nearby vent, blowing heated air into the room, gave off the only sound for several moments. Thoughts of Lia Robinson overwhelmed him.

Her name had come up in conversation numerous times because Frank Marshall had become James's second father. So, a Marshall dinner invite had become frequent over the years.

Many coveted an opportunity to enjoy their great company and even better culinary fare. After all, Jenna was a splendid cook and perfect hostess.

However, every gathering came with updates about Lia. Jenna's matchmaking attempts, as blatant as Marshall's obvious discomfort, were a testament to Jenna's unwavering determination. James' successful avoidance of meeting Lia over the years only fueled Jenna's persistence. His equally apparent demonstrations in circumventing that hazardous outcome stemmed from James' belief that men like him didn't deserve a woman like Lia Robinson.

Drawn to the photograph again, James moved a thumb across the shiny surface to rest on her plump, rosy-pink lips. In every pose he saw of her, his reaction to seeing the goodness of her spirit stayed consistent.

Like a powerful homing beacon, that face pulled him to her and clouded his focus. But James had no room for distractions.

"For Christ's sake," he cursed under his breath. Realizing that he sat there imagining the texture of her skin like a schoolboy with a crush, James clenched his jaw tighter. *I need to get my head in the fucking game.*

As he read through the information in the file, snippets of details he had heard through the Marshalls came to mind.

Lia was four years his junior. Her professional interest specialized in children's trauma. Jenna had often described Lia's talent as a calling. Having graduated from Stanford early at eighteen with a Ph.D. in childhood behavioral development, Frank figured Lia's intelligence would take her places.

Like many other predictions regarding Lia, Frank had been on point.

In under two years, Lia obtained her doctorate in trauma disorders and traveled worldwide in both her professional capacity and charity endeavors.

Unfortunately, Lia's father died when she was eleven, so he never saw the wonderful woman she had become. But Frank Marshall did, and since having met John Robinson in college, he remained friends long afterward and took his role as Lia's godfather very seriously.

Frank watched as James flipped through the pages in the file that Marshall had expediently obtained. The large stack of information took less than an hour to compile after Michelle Robinson called and informed him of Lia's capture. At the end of the report, Frank clipped the ransom note sent to Lia's mother late last night onto the back inside cover.

Suddenly, James raised his head, and their gazes clashed. "What the hell does the ransom note mean?"

The older man just shook his head from side to side. He sighed heavily and said, "I was hoping you could find out."

James

Chapter Three

Present Day

Lia placed the plastic jug beside the bed. "Well, a bed is putting it mildly," she whispered to James, referring to the crude pallet of straw with a scratchy, moth-eaten blanket on top. Despite its humble nature, she was grateful, knowing it was a little more than lying on the ground; it was better than nothing. She sighed. "More importantly, we're safe for the time being."

Two days had passed since dragging James out of the enemy's territory. His survival, hanging by a thread, made every decision more crucial. Several times, he had teetered on the brink of death, requiring every ounce of strength and essence she could pour into him. Their minds and spirits were now irreversibly entwined, encapsulating him in the land of the living.

She remained resolute, refusing to let the Angel of Death claim another lost soul. At least, that was what James called himself, and he had tried adamantly to use that lost soul excuse to keep an emotional distance from her initially.

"But I say you're not lost anymore. I found you," she promised the injured warrior, lovingly stroking his jawline. Lia claimed her Destiny wholeheartedly.

"Destiny," Lia sighed.

That word had held little meaning to her until she met this very stubborn, complex man. As their eyes met, their lives became irrevocably intertwined in that crystallizing moment.

Not now—or ever—could she, would she, lose him to death and remain unscathed.

Although, from what Tanger had said in both broken English and Mazatecan, she suspected that particular possibility couldn't happen. *Now.*

As an empath, Lia's powerful ability had always worked passively. She never used it in an intrusive, aggressive manner. However, when pushed to the extreme, her unique talent could accomplish much more than she had ever imagined.

"And this week has been very extreme," she huffed faintly.

Even now, realizing what her actions had inadvertently done, she would do it all again. She just hoped James would understand.

Carefully easing up from the pallet, she moved to James' reclined body. The bowl with icy water began losing its cooling temperature in the afternoon heat. She squeezed the excess water from the rag. Knowing that these mock sponge baths kept the fever down to a manageable degree made them a necessary task, no matter how sleep-deprived she became.

The cloth trailed the contours of his sharp, angular features—a face that most would describe as more compelling than handsome. With her empty hand, she combed her fingers through the strands resting along his broad forehead. His deep chestnut brown hair, with reddish highlights, needed a haircut, but these wavy, thick locks would tempt any woman to explore.

A small smile appeared along Lia's mouth. Knowing James these past days, she suspected the highlights definitely didn't come from a salon. She brushed another strand away from his face and moved the wet rag over his forehead.

James softly mumbled in approval and leaned into her hand, holding the rag.

She bent over him and softly kissed his dry, cracked lips. When she returned upright, a trembling spread throughout her frame. Exhaustion took its toll. The hot rag returned to the bowl as she prepared to repeat the cooling ministrations.

Tanger, this remote area's medical expert, was reverently called 'Curandero' by the villagers. The closest translation meant medicine man. Although seemingly ancient in appearance, he still insisted on joining in on the search, and once finding James, he stayed on to help.

"A life debt, much owed. Helped village from evil men," he had said. No persuasion could deter him from helping her. In her opinion, Tanger had more than paid the debt back in full because time became the most valuable commodity in James' survival.

Having delivered this precious cold water from the nearby river himself, the healer had assured her that the patient would survive. Before leaving them alone again, he had said something about getting more Anis for James' tonic.

Even though Lia understood only half of what Tanger said, his actions more than made up for the language barrier.

Her petite frame shuddered in remembrance of how close they had come to losing James.

When. Not if, James wakes up, Lia thought before her posture stiffened. No doubt, she would have a few choice words to share with him when he woke up for scaring her like that.

The two most poignant points shouted in her mind:

How dare he sacrifice himself like that?!

Did he not understand how lost I'd be without him?

A shaky exhale escaped her lips. "But that didn't happen," Lia muttered softly, as if saying the words out loud put more power toward his present situation and keeping a favorable diagnosis for the future.

They had found James just in time, his life hanging by a thread, which tethered to Lia. Tanger, with his quick administrations, had cauterized the more severe wounds to halt the internal bleeding. The herbs—that Tanger just happened to bring along, which they had forced James to drink continually—were the only thing keeping the worst of the infection at bay.

In addition, and holding no less importance, the healer's gentle demeanor and thoughtful companionship had kept her glued together during the worst of James' injuries.

The swishing sound of fabric brought her around swiftly.

A significant presence stepped into the small one-room structure, a long dark scarf wrapped around the man's head. The fabric obstructed his face, except for his eyes. His brilliant, crystal-blue eyes—mirroring James'—flared brightly between the drab cloth.

"I've managed transport out tonight. Your godfather will have someone rendezvous with us in the mountains for medical extraction." Josh Patterson, James' younger brother, began unwrapping his headgear. The similarities between the two brothers stopped at eye color and body build.

Josh's severe haircut accentuated his sharp features. His hair color was a stark contrast to that of his older brother, who had more auburn with chestnut streaks. A carefully sculpted goatee, the same color as his hair, outlined his sharp cheekbones and bowlike lips. His striking eyes, with a playful glint, dominated all his other features. His appearance and demeanor were so disarming that he could easily pass for anything other than a soldier—perhaps even a male model.

Having done a quick stint of modeling in college, Lia remained familiar with those kinds of looks and what came with them. She hadn't been impressed with most of her associates in her youth. His relaxed temperament reminded Lia of those immature men. Plus, growing up with strong male role models like her dad, Frank Marshall, and then meeting James, Josh's temperament had surprised Lia.

Thinking his cavalier attitude would get them killed and lumping the younger brother in with the self-conceited youths of her past, Lia hadn't taken kindly to him when they first met. Little did she know, her initial judgment of him was about to be turned on its head.

It didn't take long for Lia to realize that beneath Josh's playful, casual demeanor lay an intense, predatory soldier—a soldier she had come to rely on, realizing their survival hinged on his skills and instincts. Her fears of James dying in this unforgiving jungle significantly lessened within the first hour of their reunion.

A reunion foretold to Lia by the village healer's **day-walking** vision a few moments before the giant's arrival came rushing into their tiny tent a day and a half ago.

Understandably, Lia's emotional turmoil at the time was palpable; the weight of the precarious situation had made her rapidly beating heart feel like it would explode out of her chest. The only reason her shaking hands hadn't pulled the trigger on James' gun was that those same colored eyes—a family trait—had stared back into hers.

Well, that, and Josh's grin was disarming, which delayed the shot, allowing Josh to grab the gun.

Soon afterward, it became plain they wouldn't have managed to get James nearly as far as they did without this friendly giant. Even with Tanger's willingness to help and knowledge of the surrounding terrain, she and the elderly medicine man couldn't had gotten James' large frame through treacherous foot trails unseen and in such a quick manner. Josh's expert help got them to this safe, small hut just in time, and no doubt, he would do the same for tonight's rendezvous.

The villagers, freed from the tyranny, were extremely thankful. But unfortunately for Lia, there wasn't much they could do to help. Taking what little remained of their possessions, they disappeared before the drug lord sent more thugs.

Although James had taken out anyone who would have tried to follow them, this maniacal group still had followers remaining in adjacent parts, who would come to investigate.

Anyone they crossed in their path would experience repercussions for their destroyed drug-harvesting camp.

Tanger wasn't the only one wanting to pay back a life debt. Lia, too, owed the Patterson brothers for getting her out of that hellhole. James' arrival shortly after her capture prevented the worst from happening, but she still experienced the depravity of evil men that would haunt her dreams for years to come.

That's if sleep became manageable at all. She had only gotten more than two consecutive hours of sleep since being captured.

Josh crossed over to where James lay resting, breaking Lia out of her musings. He watched as her body jerked when he came too close. While his face held a neutral expression, he quickly stepped back and raised his hands in surrender. But the hut remained small; there wasn't much distance to gain.

"Why don't you take a few hours to rest? I will tend to my brother."

Lia nodded and turned away. The last several days had tested her faith in people's good intentions, but she clung to a flicker of hope. A flustering heat infused her face and neck. She bent down and eased her body onto the second pallet on the opposite wall. In this perilous situation, she couldn't ignore the existence of evil men. But just as clear, if not more so, she had witnessed the extent of goodness, too. Extraordinary men existed—good men who stood up against this evil to defend the helpless, inspiring her with their courage.

Rolling onto her back, she rested an arm over her eyes to block out the brightness in the room. Lia hadn't had the time nor inclination to figure out much around her other than James' continuing improvement. But she'd never been exposed to people like her as much as these past few days. Even Tanger's strange abilities seemed commonplace in this obscure area, with all the villagers' casual acceptance of what he could do.

How had he known where to look for James that night precisely?

Or why hadn't he been surprised by Josh Patterson's abrupt appearance the following day?

Nor had he frowned upon James' self-healing ability.

All of those silent questions made her head swim. She didn't know what to make of it, and a giant sigh escaped. Sleep would not come. Instead, she found herself drawn into a deep reflection on the past days, her mind fully engaged with the events that had unfolded.

Chapter Four

Day after kidnapping

A continuous humming nearby brought Lia out of a deep sleep. She woke up on a small cot in the corner of a massive storage structure. Easing up, she rested on her forearm in a semi-reclined position and massaged her aching head.

At first, her mind remained sluggish, but that soon got pushed away by blind panic. The visual study of the surrounding area was a stark contrast to her familiar bedroom. This was not a place she recognized, and she had no memory of how she got here or where exactly **here** was.

A quick survey of the surrounding area and of her reclined form only fueled her confusion.

She had no idea how many building levels were above her, but the ceiling was at least ten feet tall. The exposed structural framing and corrugated metal sheeting could be the roof or another floor above. Her eyes darted to the numerous linear fluorescent lamps hung from wires suspended from the metal framing. These lights were the source of the consistent humming that had roused her to full wakefulness.

Plus, the heat in the room was stifling.

The walls around her were comprised of concrete masonry blocks and looked aged with time. The concrete floor went without paint, but a slight sheen adhered to the surface. Lia's gaze traveled to multiple areas with dark reddish-brown splatters on the walls and floors.

Her attention jumped and stayed fixed on a large, stained, condensed area surrounding a small metal chair. This chair was anchored in place by thick metal brackets fastened to both the chair's legs and the concrete floor.

A deep, shuddering wave of fear engulfed Lia, rendering her vulnerable. She couldn't even bring herself to imagine what those stains might signify.

"Where on earth am I?" she whispered, her voice lost in the oppressive silence as she continued to scrutinize her surroundings, her confusion deepening.

On one of the longer-length walls stood rows of large wooden crates parallel to the wall. Those crates were stacked three high and had a total of eight rows. The opposite wall had heavy-duty industrial shelves, back-to-back, positioned perpendicular to the wall. Four units lined the wall with a wide aisleway between each row. Lastly, at the short end of the building stood three hangar doors spaced evenly. Old, dirty cardboard sheets blocked the single glass windows centered on each door.

Lia sat up and attempted to lower her legs to the ground, only to be halted by a sudden resistance in her left leg. Her feet, bare and vulnerable, were encircled by a metal manacle. Her gaze followed the short length of the chain, which ended at a heavy-duty ring mounted on the wall about four feet from the floor, emphasizing her physical restraint.

Her breathing became harsh and loud. The beating of her heart in her chest seemed to thud within her head. The metal ring secured the length of the chain with a padlock. The size of the chain allowed only a short radius away from the metal ring.

Lia quickly braced her feet against the wall and pulled with all her might. But the chain did not break.

Suddenly, a large man came through a door. Lia's eyes flew to the automatic rifle that swung from a belt and wrapped around his shoulder and back as he entered and stopped inches from the cot.

His grin held a malicious promise. He grabbed the metal links and tugged with forceful strength, bringing her leg off the bed's surface. He continued to pull the chain tight, straining the connection between the ring and the anchor around her ankle.

This action dragged her from the cot until just her upper back kept her on the flat surface.

Without any words spoken, he did his best to make his meaning crystal clear.

No matter how hard he pulled, the chain and ring would not disconnect. Then he stopped and tossed the excess chain at her reclining form. The chain's weight and speed of the toss knocked the breath from her lungs when it hit her stomach.

The man just chuckled at her grimace of pain. He turned his back on her and walked out, not before turning off the switch by the door and leaving her in complete darkness.

Only later that evening did Lia discover that two sets of keys could free her from the moored prison.

One key belonged to the chief guard, Carlos—the charming man who had come in after she woke up here. Although he took pleasure in tormenting Lia, the fearful respect he had toward the other key holder kept him from doing anything else.

That man, Raul Ortego, had introduced himself later that night when he brought in a bucket of drinking water. Her unique empathic ability sensed evil in both of these individuals, but Raul's presence instilled a fear in Lia unlike any she had experienced before.

Despite her obedience, Raul's relentless slaps continued to happen. His sparse Spanish commands, devoid of any emotion, were met with her compliance, but no matter how quickly she obeyed, it was never enough. Raul's enjoyment of inflicting pain was evident, and Lia's resilience was beginning to waver.

At first, the mandates he had given were purposely degrading and uncomfortable for someone with a modest upbringing, but nothing to put her life in jeopardy. But subsequently, each time afterward, their taunts became more explicit, more cutting—designed to break her spirit.

Each time, following those interactions, their touches became more invasive, bruising, and cruel—designed to increase her fear.

She had no idea what they wanted. So far, all of her requests for information went either unanswered or resulted in another hard slap. Lia knew her present captors were waiting for someone to show up before anything truly happened. This increased her dread astronomically each time someone burst through the door.

Lia had a terrible feeling she wouldn't leave this place unscathed.

James

Chapter Five

The second day after the kidnapping

Late that afternoon, a Ford Bronco came barreling in, startling Lia from a short nap. The middle garage door rocked on its metal track as the vehicle stopped just inside the opening, a yard from Lia's cot. Two men dressed in soldiers' dark green and black camo fatigues exited from the front driver's and passenger's sides of the vehicle. They both headed to the truck's back compartment.

She watched as a man was dragged from the vehicle's storage trunk. A coarse, dark-colored fabric hood covered his head as they hauled him to a chair—the same chair fastened to the concrete floor.

Oh no, Lia thought to herself in horror. Her heartbeat sped up to an alarming degree. The thought of becoming a witness to the vile actions that had resulted in those floor stains from previous altercations almost made her faint.

With increasing dread, powerless to do anything to stop it, she watched as they tied the man's hands behind his back. From what Lia could make out, heavy-duty zip ties fastened them together.

Shoving the prisoner down hard onto that menacing object, the soldiers secured the new arrival to that horrible chair by linking another zip tie through the bound wrists to the metal chair's back post.

Lia recognized only one of the men—Carlos, the chief prison guard. The other man she'd never seen before. That man went to the industrial shelves and pulled down two metal folding chairs. He handed one of the chairs to Carlos, opened the remaining chair, and set it close to the new prisoner.

In contrast, Carlos positioned himself alongside the prisoner to the left.

Carlos turned toward Lia and shouted in broken English for her to turn and face the corner. He also warned her that if he saw her face in their direction again, she would be severely hurt.

While Carlos threatened Lia, the other man grinned and spoke in a jeering manner to his counterpart. Lia couldn't understand a word of the loud, rapid-fire delivery of nasal-sounding words that shot from his mouth like a machine gun firing.

Lia spoke Spanish fluently. Her mother was an immigrant from Mexico. Although Michelle Robinson embraced her adopted country and reflected most Americana mannerisms, she ensured Lia knew of her Mexican heritage.

Mixtec or Nahuatl, maybe? Lia had thought, knowing that other languages were spoken in Mexico other than Spanish. But it didn't matter. The end result was a language barrier, difficult to translate. Still, her empathic ability allowed her to pick up a hint of their meaning nonetheless.

Lia tucked close to the wall, making her body as small as possible. Tears seeped from tightly closed lids, saturating the thin cloth of the mattress.

Carlos turned back toward his partner and shoved him hard, proving dominance between them. He gave a low warning growl to the other soldier before directing his attention to the male prisoner. Whipping out his hand, Carlos roughly grabbed the hood and ripped it off.

James Patterson blinked dry eyelids several times, letting the audience soak in his fake identity's phony nuances. He jerked his gaze from one soldier to the other, not keeping direct eye contact with either man for long.

"What's going on here? Why did you grab me? I'm an American citizen on a relief aid mission affiliated with the Red Cross. People will be looking for me!"

This announcement only bored the two guards. They continued studying the American aid worker. By the prisoner's appearance, they assumed they were dealing with an administrator who was used to supervising rather than accomplishing any physical labor. His clothes had looked new, pressed, and immaculate when he was snatched, but now they showed rips, smears, dirt, and blood.

"You should let me go!" the American arrogantly yelled.

Carlos swiftly stood up and sent a brutal punch to the man's stomach. "Shut it, Gringo, and hear. You don't come in me country and say shots. I do," he sneered with satisfaction. He had finally gotten the chance to dole out some hurt that he couldn't accomplish with the woman.

Unfortunately, it didn't provide the same degree of gratification for this type of man, but it was something.

Carlos kicked the man several times with vicious force upon the lower limbs and ankles. Reaching out and grasping the man's mouth, he squeezed hard, pressing his lips tightly together and cutting off the moans of pain emitted from them. "You shut mouth—take what I give. Or I give more bad."

James quickly nodded, Carlos's fingers still painfully squeezing his lips. He gave the captors—what they wanted—the submission to their authority.

"Now, me ask truths." The younger soldier grinned, enjoying the prisoner's easy capitulation. "These Americanos need to be put in proper place. Think much of themselves," he said with a heavier accent. He jerked his chin toward their prisoner and, for good measure, kicked the nearest leg of the man's chair. "Now, give true answer, and get life."

The prisoner nodded again, this time more quickly.

Still facing the corner, Lia's eyes squeezed tightly closed. She had a good guess about what was happening, but using her ability would reveal the true depths of their depravity.

Flaring her empathic telepathy wide open, Lia absorbed the feelings all around her—their hatred toward the American, the sadistic pleasure in inflicting pain, the satisfaction of dominating another helpless person, and the glee they felt when blatantly lying to the man. None of what she sensed from those two soldiers surprised Lia.

They had no intention of letting that man live past the night. Remorse did not weigh on their hearts at all. Instead, they relished the opportunity to cause this man deadly harm.

The sharp, intense, and feverish vibrations flowing from these villains felt no different from her first contact. Sometimes, the sensations worsened, and the fiery burn seemed to encapsulate Lia's mind completely, but for now, these familiar sensations were becoming manageable.

However, surprise nearly made her gasp aloud when a wave of feelings shot from the prisoner's mind into hers.

Lia had expected terror. She had prepared herself to handle that frigid coldness—that blunt pulling pain in her head. But what she felt instead burned hot. It was like a knife slicing through raw meat with fierce speed and strength.

A sharp clarity and a predatory calculation shot out from him.

A small gasp did escape her pressed lips this time.

Lia, are you hurt? A crisp, authoritative voice broke through her mental shields.

Who is this? Lia sent her message back through the connection.

Answer me, the voice impatiently ordered, then added, *Are you injured?*

I... I'm- uh, fine.

Good. Can you run fast for a mile or two?

Yes, I think so-

No guessing. Tell me if you can or cannot, the voice insisted.

Yes. I can. Lia suspected that the man tied to the chair was speaking to her through a telepathic connection. *Who are you?*

"Hey! Give truth, Gringo! Who give medical stuff took with Bronco? More there?" Carlos demanded an answer. The glint in his eyes reflected unrelenting greed for money and power. Knowing this prisoner would provide the means to cash, Carlos would handle the rest from there.

James hesitated at first.

Seeing the avoidance, Carlos struck the leg of James' chair repeatedly in rapid succession. "No ask again!" He pulled out a large switchblade from his back pocket and tilted the blade from side to side. The light from the overhead industrial lamps flashed on the smooth metal surface of the sharp edge.

James rapidly nodded his head up and down, keeping his attention on the swaying knife.

The younger guard grinned with anticipation and asked, "Village? Picked Gringo up?" His voice was eager at the possibility of added bounty.

Carlos swung his palm out and struck the prisoner's chin.

James let his head snap back and then slowly brought it forward. "Yes. There are two more shipments scheduled to arrive later today." He licked the blood from his lips, caused by the force of the hit against his teeth. "They were held up at the airport with customs. I, uh, with two other volunteers, came ahead to get set up at the clinic-"

"No see anyone," Carlos interrupted.

James turned gingerly and met Carlos's beady gaze before lowering his focus to the floor. "They went to the next village over in a borrowed truck. More volunteers are helping at another clinic. They had offered assistance to us but needed a ride."

"Time they come back?" Carlos asked while studying the dirt under his nails.

"Tomorrow," James answered softly. "Tomorrow, early morning."

Lia heard a tremble in the man's voice. She was sure that the guards heard only the fear, too, because they quickly dismissed their prisoner afterward with jeering disdain—calling the man an estúpido tonto (a stupid fool).

Carlos put the hood back over James' head. The force of his movements pushed the prisoner's head down toward his chest. A groan of pain escaped.

The guard sneered and pushed again at the man's covered head before laughing.

After a few moments of silence, Lia heard the two men moving further away.

Then, the scraping of pitted metal with no lubrication cut through the quiet as they manually closed the large door. She heard the heavy boots pound against the ground as the two men walked away from the building.

Squeezing her eyelids shut, Lia pushed the remaining tears from her eyes. Biting down on her swollen lips, she kept the sigh from escaping. That's when she became hopeful that she would leave this place alive.

She had a good feeling that those soldiers were the real fools. Because waves of vibrating anticipation resonated from the man tied to the chair—it felt like a volcano ready to blow.

Lia kept very still, her face tucked into the corner until the sound of the guards' footsteps receded. When she turned back around, she blinked several times, adjusting to the light again. She spotted the man tied to the chair.

He slowly tilted his head from side to side while his shoulders shifted up and down several times.

"What are you doing?" Lia asked in a low whisper.

Don't talk. The voice sounded brisk and cold inside her mind. *Just communicate telepathically.*

Lia quickly looked at the small monitoring device mounted above the door. The small perimeter around the cot would be visible to the guards.

Who are you? Lia scooted off the edge of the cot and stood beside the bed. Her scrutiny remained fixed on the man with unease.

My name is James Patterson...

Chapter Six

Lia recognized his name. Her godmother often spoke about the severely dedicated soldier in Frank Marshall's unit, but she had never met him in person.

Is it one and the same? Her thoughts slipped out.

Yes. The same. Your godfather sent me, James replied telepathically.

You don't look like you have the situation under control. Lia sank back down onto the cot and slowly shook her head from side to side.

It's all part of the plan.

Lia felt, rather than saw, his smirk hidden by the hood covering his face.

Of course. I never doubted it for a minute. Lia's response was dripping with doubt. *Seriously, can you fill me in on the plan?*

James sighed loudly and adjusted his large frame on the small chair. *When do they plan on killing me?*

Lia couldn't help the exclamation that escaped before whispering, "How did you know?" His earlier command became forgotten when surprise had her speaking out loud.

Don't talk, James reprimanded swiftly.

Sorry, Lia sent back. *How did you know that I could tell what they planned?*

She wasn't used to others knowing about her unique abilities. Frank Marshall often reminded her and her mother not to disclose those abilities to anyone.

Frank Marshall told me about you when I agreed to bring you home. If you couldn't tell— I have unique talents too. Usually, I can only talk telepathically like this with my brothers and sister. But I felt our connection when I came in. It must have something to do with your empathic talent. Frank suspects that your abilities made you a target.

But how would they even know about them? I've never told anyone. No one has said anything about why I'm even here, Lia informed him.

Did they ask for anything? James clarified.

No. Nothing. Lia quickly replied. *I get the sense that they are waiting for someone else—*

There's definitely someone else, James interrupted. *Those bozos aren't smart enough to come up with a plan unless an opportunity presents itself.*

Like you and your caravan of supplies? Lia interjected.

Exactly, James replied.

What they lack in intelligence, they make up for in venom. You don't want to mess with those guys without backup. Lia's hand lifted, and she rubbed the side of her jaw with a light touch. The bruises from past encounters with Raul stood sharp against her creamy-caramel complexion.

Don't worry about my backup. Just be ready to bolt when I tell you.

Right. Sure. When you give me the go-ahead. Lia's hand moved from her face and gripped the links in the chain to rattle them quickly. *Oh right. I seem to be shackled to the wall, which makes bolting anywhere a problem.*

Got that covered. When were they going to try to get rid of me?

Tonight. Lia's thought sighed with worry.

When? James pushed.

It's not like my empathic abilities can be that precise regarding future intentions. People typically don't plan down to a minute or an hour.

I do, James clarified.

Well, Carlos and that man with him didn't.

Uh. Too bad. I was hoping you could. That way, I can get my brothers set up.

Do you mean they aren't already? Lia asked. Her level of frustration transferred through their telepathic connection.

Not quite. They're in the... vicinity. They're ready for multiple scenarios, but narrowing our exit strategy according to the most likely outcome would be better.

Again... Didn't you do that already? Lia repeated herself.

James tilted his head and waited a few moments before replying. *I don't recall Frank mentioning how difficult you could be.*

And I don't recall my godfather mentioning how unprepared you were during your missions. He often said you and your brothers were the best. If getting captured is your best... Lia left that sentence unfinished.

James released a loud, drawn-out sigh.

Lia heard the barely-there comment, "It's gonna be a long night," and was about to agree with him when suddenly the single door opened and slammed against the wall.

Shrieking at the sudden loud crashing sound, Lia turned toward the doorway. Raul came strutting in and approached the cot in three long strides. He turned slightly and glanced toward James. His grin reflected a sinister intent. "Carlos told me we had a visitor."

Raul immediately dismissed the other prisoner, restrained at the bolted-down chair, and turned back toward Lia.

"Carlos and Alejandro left with a handful of men to provide a welcome party to the remaining volunteers and the supplies they bring. It's just you and me with a handful of my men, who are all loyal to me. There will be no interruptions."

Raul's present speech held more words than all their combined dialogue since Lia's arrival.

Lia's body trembled violently. His English came across flawlessly with a lyrical accent. The evil gleam that reflected in his stare terrified her. But it was nothing compared to the thick, oozing weight that began to coat her mind.

"I can finally pay you a proper visit before my boss arrives. You should play nice if you want to survive."

Realizing that her future survival depended on surrendering to all manners of his vile advances should have made her compliance understandable. But that wasn't what came out of her mouth. "I will fight you with every breath," Lia swore, trembling with a fear so palpable it took over her body.

Raul's smile became wider, convincing Lia that he had been hoping for a fight. His sneering comment, "So be it. That makes it all the more fun for me," confirmed it.

"I'm sure I can explain your injuries, Senorita, without too much difficulty," he further explained before advancing toward her. But his arms and upper body had the only momentum of motion.

Raul's eyes flashed wide open as his mouth formed a perfect *O*. His gaze flickered toward his legs, then quickly went back to Lia's face. "What manner of magic is this?" he growled, struggling to make his lower body move forward, but he remained frozen in place.

Lia felt tiny, sharp, stabbing prickles of coldness pierce her shields. Raul's fear blasted into her mind. Accustomed to these reactions, she instinctively reinforced her shields to counter the physical discomfort.

A movement nearby tore her eyes away from Raul. Lia gasped in amazement as her godfather's soldiers stood up from the stationary chair. He snapped apart the zip ties securing his wrists and yanked the hood off his head.

Even understanding their perilous situation didn't stop her fascination as James approached them, making no sound in his movements. However, the look on his face made Lia thankful he was on her side.

Still caught up in the struggle to move, Raul remained unaware of how death stalked closer, his fate sealed when he threatened Lia. With a full, swift sweep of James' arm, Raul flew across the room.

Death became the immediate result when Raul's body slammed brutally hard against a solid wall.

Lia followed the path of Raul's flight and then squeezed her eyes shut when his body sagged to the floor.

But a tug on the mooring's leash had her eyes flashing open again. James gently moved the chain clear of her body before holding it taut against the metal ring attached to the wall. Lia heard a pop of metal snap, and then the links dropped free from the ring. She saw James' hand flash forward, catching the chain before it landed near her.

Lia's gaze involuntarily went to Raul before switching back to her leash. "He has the key," she softly said.

James' attention locked onto her as he replied, "I won't need it." While advancing toward her slowly, he gestured toward her foot. A cautious look morphed into a relieved expression when Lia extended her leg without hesitation.

He gently picked up her foot, holding the arch of it in his warm palm.

Lia shivered with awareness.

James felt the involuntary movement, and his scrutiny held her captive as effectively as the chain. Lia lowered her gaze to the foot of the cot, breaking the strange spell. When she felt her ankle's release from the metal cuff, she tried tucking her foot closer to her body.

At first, James didn't let go. Instead, he traced the redness where the manacle had rubbed against her skin. His touch seemed to heat her from the outside in, and her face and upper body flushed with a pink tone.

Waves of awareness ebbed and flowed around them like the pull of the tides caused by the moon. This unstoppable pull surged and echoed within her mind and body. Biting down gently, Lia held in a gasp between closed lips.

This strange connection felt unlike anything she had ever experienced before. But now wasn't the time to figure out why. They needed to escape.

Chapter Seven

Present Day

Lia woke suddenly, and the gasp she held in during that dream immediately escaped. She sprang up from her reclined position.

Josh Patterson quickly backed up, raising his hands, palms facing out toward Lia. His gentle nudge to wake her hadn't turned out as planned, but with everything that had happened so far, Josh understood Lia's reaction.

"We're ready to move." He gestured toward the opening and then swung his glance back. "Can you carry the supply pack?"

With a determined look in her eyes, Lia pushed off the floor and headed for the duffel bag near James' reposed form. She grunted with the effort of lifting the weighty pack, but her resolve remained fixed. Swinging it over her head, she secured it in place, repositioning the strap so it lay across her chest and rested the bag crosswise against her back.

While Lia took care of the pack, Josh came closer to handle moving James.

Josh's sudden movement caused Lia's body to tense up momentarily, but she quickly forced herself to relax her shoulders and breathing.

Josh had stopped instantly. Taking his cue, when Lia's stance eased, he started again, this time much slower. When he reached James, he carefully lifted his brother's relaxed frame and positioned him in a fireman's hold.

Josh turned and faced Lia. "We'll need to move quickly."

Lia's response was a single, solemn nod. Then a question hung in the air, spoken with heavy concern. "Did Tanger come back? Is he"—?"

"Tanger is waiting for us. He'll guide us to the mountain peak and then head back down to meet the rest of his family." Josh lifted his chin and angled toward the makeshift doorway. "We're wasting daylight. I want to get close to the peak before sunset. If the skies are clear, we should have close to a full moon to help us. But I don't want to take that chance."

Josh's voice held steady, his caution palpable considering the situation. He wanted to be prepared for anything.

Lia didn't waste any more time responding. She felt the vibration of Josh's urgency projecting into her mind in swift, repetitive waves. Lia wasn't sure if Josh's emotions were due to the severity of his brother's injuries or the possible dire situation they were heading into. Knowing either was reason enough, she cleared the doorway's threshold as her gaze searched the nearby area.

Tanger wasn't far from the hut's opening when Lia stepped out. The storage structure she exited from had been used by the villagers for one of the lingering coffee plantation's drying processes. It had been a godsend since harvesting wouldn't occur for another few weeks.

Lia's gaze rested upon the satchel Tanger carried among several other canvas bags tied and looped around his body. The various herbs and concoctions that filled Tanger's precious handbags had kept James alive and somewhat comfortable these past days.

Having spotted Lia's focused gaze, Tanger patted the bag holding all her attention. He grinned and nodded his head up and down. "Good pickings," he said, using broken English. "Keep bad germs go." His attention shifted to the tall giant exiting the hut. "Go. Now."

Tanger's head bounced quickly before turning his back on them and striding out of their makeshift camp.

Lia felt the same waves of urgency emanating from Tanger, just like Josh's. *Oh God, please let us get out of here. Please let James be okay.* She prayed frantically.

Lia looked sideways and caught Josh's 'go after him' gesture. Not needing any more prompting, she quickly moved in place behind Tanger, and their journey was once again in motion.

The day's heat refused to ease into cooler temperatures. Even though the canopy of foliage swung overhead—blocking the direct sunlight—the air held the moist heat like a sauna. Lia felt her lungs getting saturated from the humidity, and every breath weighed uncomfortably heavy.

As the sun sank lower, the volume of the surrounding wildlife increased, their calls rising in a growing chorus. The noises were unlike anything she had heard before. They pierced her eardrums. However, the sudden silence each time the group got closer to whatever had made those noises became even more nerve-wracking. Knowing their proximity to each other could likely bring unwelcome surprises made it hard to enjoy the quiet.

Every step of this brisk, relentless trek only served to heighten Lia's fears, yet she pressed on. The knowledge of what was at stake fueled her determination, refusing to let her fears overpower her.

No matter how rough the terrain became, Lia kept close to Tanger as ordered. She ignored the stinging bug bites and the cooling temperatures as night approached. Her eyes stayed on

Tanger's limbering figure for over an hour and a half while centering her empathic connection with James.

As James slept, his mind remained a quiet void. Nonetheless, Lia found solace in the fact that he was still alive, a reassuring presence in the midst of uncertainty.

When the steep incline of their path loomed in the fading light, Lia's voice, barely above a whisper, broke the silence. "Are we there yet?"

Her words hung in the air, a childlike quip used on many long car rides, meant to break the tangible tension in the fast-approaching darkness.

Lia heard Josh's chuckle before Tanger suddenly stopped and turned around.

"We're good," he replied, his ever-present grin spreading across his face. "Make top in—" Tanger held up two fingers on his right hand, shifting them several times, first with his palm facing downward, then tilting upward.

Taking his hand gesture to mean "so-so," Lia didn't have the energy to question him further.

"We go, hurry," Tanger instructed. He turned back, facing forward, and continued at a fast pace that didn't seem possible given his age.

Lia allowed a slight groan to escape before sucking it back in.

"We go, hurry," Josh repeated in a soft voice before releasing another chuckle.

It took too much effort for Lia to chuckle back. Instead, she switched her focus back to Tanger's back and, internally, to James's life force. Those were the only two things she concentrated on as she took one step after another for the next three and a half hours.

By the end of that trek, her mind remained linked to James, but little else registered. She barely remembered meeting their extraction team. Everything blurred through exhaustion and worry. When Josh's voice penetrated the fog of her mind—so devoted to James's survival—she didn't take notice at first. His insistent tone and forceful shaking finally broke through her awareness.

"Lia, let go," Josh demanded, trying to pull her hand from James so the medics could work on him.

She blinked as multiple hands tugged at her. When they finally managed to pry her away, she stumbled and sank to the ground. The harsh edges of rocks digging into her knees and hands went unnoticed.

Suddenly, strong arms lifted her. Her legs dangled over Josh's right arm while his left arm cradled her back. "You did it," he said while carrying her out of the team's way as they rushed to stabilize James's condition.

"My brother's chances of making it out of here alive are possible thanks to you," Josh whispered in her ear. "Now, get some rest."

Lia didn't remember anything else. Her eyes closed, and sleep swept her under.

Chapter Eight

A couple of days later, James slept in shorter stretches as he continued recovering from surgery. The previous night, the surgeon had admitted his shock during a post-surgery follow-up, marveling that James had survived so many serious injuries. With an uncanny rate of accelerated healing, his rapid improvement continued to amaze the hospital staff, as well as Lia. But his brothers, unwavering in their confidence in James, took his progress in stride, expecting nothing less from their powerful sibling.

Although Lia had been admitted alongside James upon arrival at the hospital, she was discharged soon afterward. Once the medical staff had treated her minor bruises and abrasions and replenished her fluids with an IV, there was no medical reason for her to stay.

After being discharged, Lia could have left with her godfather, but she chose not to. Instead, she remained by James' side, a silent but powerful presence of support.

Typically, one or two of James' brothers joined her bedside vigil. One stayed in the hospital room while the other coordinated with the guards posted throughout the hospital, and then they would switch. Lia wasn't sure whether they were guarding her or keeping her prisoner.

"Maybe it's a little of both," Frank Marshall had joked when Lia mentioned her suspicion the first night while waiting for James to get out of surgery.

Frank had stopped by that first day and stayed through the first night, but no one had seen him since. However, he continued to check in on James' progress, either through one of the brothers, Lia, or by phone.

Each time James awoke, he became more aware of his surroundings—especially of the growing connection with Lia, a bond that strengthened with each passing moment.

So when hushed whispers nearby wrenched James from a deep sleep, he immediately felt Lia stirring. *Dammit, She needs her rest!* his mind complained, and he was determined to do something about it.

James meant to whisper for whoever was talking to be quiet, but only a rumbling growl escaped his lips. He forced his heavy eyelids to lift and frowned at the two guilty-looking individuals standing beside his hospital bed.

The room was dimly lit, with only a single lamp mounted on the wall beside him. Slowly and with great care, James eased himself upright. The looks on his brothers' faces told him they had bad news to share.

James glared at them, then turned his head slightly to check on Lia. She had settled back to sleep on the small couch provided in the private suite.

That first time he had come to in the hospital, James had mistaken his surroundings for a four-star hotel. Even amidst his struggles with the staff preparing him for surgery, the room's decor didn't resemble a typical hospital setting. And when he hadn't immediately seen Lia, he had feared for her safety.

Frank Marshall had mentioned high security when James grumbled about the luxurious accommodations. Even patting James' head like a child in need of reassurance hadn't eased his mind. Then, leaning in closer, Frank had told him to let the staff do their job. But James had resisted, fighting the body's pull to surrender to unconsciousness.

It had taken Marshall's legendary *don't-push-it-or-else* glare—along with physically hauling Lia closer to his side—to do the impossible.

Only after realizing that Lia was safe had James relented, easing back down. With only the strength to nod in agreement before even that seemed like a Herculean effort, he had finally surrendered to his body's demands.

"Tell him," Sean's sharp whisper broke the stillness around them. It seemed to vibrate off the walls, gaining volume as it moved through the air.

James' gaze flicked toward Lia again. Satisfied that she was still resting, he looked back at his asinine brothers and waited.

Sean stepped closer and smacked Josh on the shoulder.

James could feel his strength returning. He eased further up on his elbows. No dizziness—no sharp pain.

So far, so good. Relief settled over him as he fumbled with the bed controls.

Sean swiped the device from his older brother and raised the bed from its flat position. Josh quickly arranged the pillows so James could recline comfortably.

James growled at their interference. "I got it," he mumbled. He turned his head on the pillow and glanced toward Lia again.

He couldn't seem to help himself.

James vaguely recalled the strange connection between them when he had first come to in Mexico with Lia tending to him. At the time, his mind had been clouded with pain and medication, so he had dismissed it as delirium.

Now, as he studied her peaceful expression in sleep, James wanted to keep it that way. She had so little rest during the ordeal. *She is still exhausted*, he reasoned to himself

His awareness of everything about her had him feeling their bond growing stronger each day, deepening beyond anything he had ever experienced—even with any of his siblings. He could sense her emotions, hear her thoughts, as if they shared the same consciousness. It was a tangible presence, like an invisible rope tethering their souls together.

James instinctively knew that whatever had happened between them—it was permanent.

He turned back to his brothers and glared. "Report," he ordered.

Josh nodded and flashed a look at his younger brother. "We have news from one of the listening devices scattered around the village and the old coffee plantation. We finally got a name. The one who ordered Lia's abduction is Amador Herrera, and he is one of the top political officials in the United Nations. His family is close to the Suarez family, with a long-standing heritage of political ties; including Upper Chamber and Senators, to be exact."

James raised a hand slightly to interrupt. "Is this tied to the Mexican government? If so..." James let it go without saying, knowing his brothers were thinking the same thing.

Those ties wouldn't be impossible to overcome; they would just be more complicated, requiring delicate maneuvering.

Josh shook his head from side to side. "No, but his family wants power and will stop at nothing to get it. There are rumors of some coup in their government."

"But why Lia?" James interrupted again.

Sean leaned closer before asking, "How much do you know about this woman?"

"Only the file I got from Frank Marshall and what he and Jenna mentioned over the years." James swiftly stole a glance toward the sofa before meeting Sean's gaze.

Sean turned his head slightly and studied the slim woman sleeping nearby. His gaze held suspicion, bringing a protective growl out of James' mouth.

A hand fisted around Sean's shirt, pulling him down within inches of James' face. "You're treading on dangerous ground," James snarled.

Sean used one hand to disengage his brother's hold and carefully eased James' hand back to rest on the bedcovers. "You don't understand. I've been looking further into Lia's background to see if there is a connection to the Herrera or Suarez families. I can't find anything," Sean said in a harsh whisper. "And I do mean—anything."

That coming from him meant a great deal. Sean was the go-to man for finding anything that someone wanted hidden.

James looked up at his brother's face and frowned. "I don't get it. That's good, right?"

"No. That's not good. There is nothing about Lia's past. She is a ghost other than the surface story that Frank Marshall had in her file. I can't get any deeper information. She has no trail to lead back to anything or anyone."

James' gaze was drawn back toward the woman lying on the sofa. His eyes followed the slim figure from her face, partially hidden, down to her feet. She had curled up into a small ball and burrowed into the pillow and covers provided for her.

"Does Frank know?" James continued to study Lia's sleeping form. Already, dread sat pitted in his stomach at what was coming next.

Chapter Nine

"I think Marshall's the cause," Sean softly said. The regret weighed heavily on his lips.

That quietly spoken information went off like a bomb inside James' head. He slowly met his brother's gaze and said, "We'll just have to see about that."

The door to James' hospital suite swung open as if speaking the words had summoned Frank Marshall into existence.

Frank stepped into the room and studied the three men, whose eyes scoped him out like they were viewing him through the barrel of a gun. These men were like sons to him. The dire situation notwithstanding, they never ceased to make him proud.

James suddenly felt a warm, thick coating of positive energy surrounding his mind. Frank's affection was like a dense, soft, comfortable blanket covering him in a physical embrace.

Bewildered by the onset of physical manifestations, James jerked upright from his reclined position, arms stretched outward. As the sensations increased, he clutched his head as if pressing against the shell of his skull would keep him from exploding outward. The sudden overflow of emotions shot through him. He was drowning in all varieties of feelings.

The machines nearby shrieked in alarm. Their shrill, beeping sounds filled the room, indicating dangerous levels of stress James was physically experiencing.

Frank quickly came forward, taking one of James' hands. Serving as an anchor, he provided a strong, steady presence for James to cling to amid the vortex of cascading emotions—something Frank had done for Lia as a child when her powers first emerged from dormancy.

James became unaware of anything other than the swarming mass of pain in his head and let out a continuous, guttural bellow. Drops of bright blood dripped from his nose onto the crisp white bedding below.

Sensing James' pain, Lia abruptly awoke. She lunged toward the hospital bed. "What the hell is going on?"

Sean and Josh tried to get to James, but Frank quickly shook his head. "Lia," Frank calmly voiced, standing amidst the chaos of shouts and tension. "Do what you can," he instructed her before focusing back on James. "Boys, keep the medical staff away. No admittance. And try to stay calm—keep your emotions steady."

Josh nodded, rushed to the door, and flipped the lock. He had no idea what Frank meant by 'calming their emotions,' but knowing Frank wouldn't mention it unless it was necessary, he concentrated on taking deep, steady breaths.

James couldn't breathe. Everything was too intense, bombarding him all at once. He couldn't separate himself from everyone else's thoughts and feelings. It was like being swept into a funneling tornado of chaos. He felt intense pain everywhere.

Fucking everywhere!

James felt multiple presences pressing on him, loading him down, burying him alive.

Suddenly, a comforting quietness settled in his mind, battling the overwhelming emotions away. Lia's voice became the only thing James wanted to be bound to in the swirling kaleidoscope of feelings.

"It's okay, honey. Just concentrate on me. Just hear my heartbeat. Match your breathing to mine." Lia inhaled long and steadily, then slowly let it out. Over and over, she repeated the process until James mimicked her meditation breathing technique. "That's it. You got it. In. Now, slowly out."

After a few moments of this deep cleansing, the machine nearby went silent.

James could feel Lia's smile—actually **feel it**. The warm touch in his mind was like facing the sun and absorbing its rays on his skin. Lia calmed the pandemonium while he latched onto this safe harbor with survival-driven intensity. She pushed the mental voices and feelings away until only she and James remained.

A sudden prick stung James' neck. Then, even Lia's presence eased from his mind, and everything faded to black.

Frank Marshall leaned back, the used needle still in his hand. Lia stood close by, but her focus remained locked on James. Only when he slumped into unconsciousness did she realize Frank had sedated him.

What the hell is going on? Lia's mind raced with that thought and a mess of others. *Why is James battling with all these emotions?* Everyone on this floor—on the entire floor above and below them—had been crammed into his head. It had been pure madness.

Stepping away, Frank Marshall placed the used needle in the hazardous waste receptacle on the wall.

Lia tenderly wiped the blood from James' face with a tissue.

Frank gestured for everyone to back away from James' side.

Shaking her head fiercely, Lia quickly disagreed. "No, I'm not leaving him! James' heart rate was beyond fast, and his blood pressure was close to stroke levels," she shouted. She moved closer to James, looking like a fierce warrior ready to strike down anyone who got near him.

Josh couldn't help but smile, even after everything that had just transpired. His admiration for Lia continued to grow. "I told you how it is between them," he said, shoving Sean in the shoulder. "She's as in the dark as the rest of us, but she's not going anywhere."

Sean growled and began pacing the length of the room. After the third pass, he stopped near Josh, sending him a silent message with just a look.

Josh gave a subtle twitch of his chin and unclenched his jaw. "She isn't leaving. What you need to say can be said right here."

Frank Marshall smiled and turned to Sean.

Sean studied the faces around him, his gaze settling back on Josh's. Reaching a conclusion, he let out a long, heavy sigh and gave in. "Okay, have it your way."

Frank chuckled, leaning back slightly, but the amusement was short-lived. What came next would bring some of his past sins into the light. "I know you boys can handle yourselves—you never cease to amaze me." He reached for Lia, pulling her gently into his arms. "But what I'm about to say will come as a shock. Just promise me you'll hear me out."

Leaning closer, Lia rested her head against Frank's chest. This man had been like a father to her since she was a teenager. Slowly, she nodded, sinking deeper into the warmth of his embrace.

A wave of sensations swept through her—an unsettling chill mixed with a dull prickling of pins and needles. Beneath that, tangled with fear and guilt, was something else—something steady and strong. A deep, endless flow of **love**.

Lia never questioned the love she felt for Frank, nor his for her. That emotion was familiar, unwavering.

But the fear? The guilt?

Those didn't belong to him. At least, not the Frank Marshall she knew.

What in the world would cause Frank Marshall to be afraid... or guilty? Lia's heart raced with a mindful concern.

Chapter Ten

L ia, deeply in love with James, stayed close to him as he slept, her hand loosely held in his—afraid to let go. Frank Marshall had a lot to answer for, but this current predicament wasn't one of them.

With the Patterson brothers' aid, her godfather had whisked them away from the hospital with his usual efficiency. What would have been a lengthy journey to the capital for an ordinary person, Frank had managed to turn into a swift relocation to a safe house three states away.

And whatever he had pushed into James' bloodstream back at the hospital had kept him out and resting comfortably the entire trip.

Her godfather had done well with this hideaway, too.

Quiet, secluded, and with access to Wi-Fi—it was everything a hermit could want.

Lia had never considered escaping her life before, but after the recent events—the betrayal, the danger that had suddenly engulfed her—living life as a hermit didn't seem so bad.

Although, the place could have had a better name. **Slaughter Beach** didn't exactly inspire a sense of safety. But Frank had assured them she and James would be secure here, at least until they could figure out what was going on.

She found herself caught in a world of brutality and intrigue, pushed beyond her physical endurance, thrown far outside her comfort zone.

Hell, most people's comfort zones.

That reassuring thought made an excellent point—especially when she considered the small matter of her soulmate appearing in the mix.

How do you return to normal when everything has gone so far beyond your typical experience?

She had to find the answer to that question—fast. She also had to figure out how to integrate new threads into the already completed, meticulously planned tapestry of her life.

Or a more pressing concern escaped, *What if two separate tapestries now have to become one?*

Brushing her free hand along James' brow, Lia pushed a few strands of hair away from his eyes. Struggling to find a way forward after what she had learned today didn't seem possible.

Her godfather had been the rock she and her mother had clung to when everything around them had turned to shifting sand. But now, discovering that the man she loved and trusted had fabricated **everything** she knew about herself—

It didn't sit well.

James' hand twitched in hers.

She slowly stood up, leaning over his still form. Despite all the uncertainty surrounding her present, she knew this man was her future.

As Lia looked at James, a surge of hope for forgiveness filled her. She had unknowingly caused him pain, and she prayed he would find it in his heart to forgive her.

This empathic ability was a double-edged sword. It had the power to destroy her lover if she didn't find a way to teach him control. She hadn't been the best pupil when she first discovered her ability as a teenager, but Frank Marshall's patience and steady hand had made it work.

Lia would do **no less** for the man she loved.

James' eyes flickered open. His gaze, at first foggy, quickly sharpened as he took in his surroundings.

His eyes darted everywhere.

The high, exposed ceiling of bleached white wood was a sight of pure beauty. A whole wall of windows, like a portal to paradise, provided no barrier to the bright sun streaming in or the splendor of the scenery beyond.

Shifting his focus closer, James realized he was lying on a large bed. The frame was part of a built-in wall unit that spanned most of the room's length. Thick posts and stretcher frames formed a canopy.

His gaze mesmerized by the sheer netting, swaying back and forth in a slow, hypnotic rhythm. Then, his eyes flicked upward, drawn to the ceiling fan—large leaf-shaped blades spinning in slow, lazy circles.

The heavy fog of the sedative finally lifted from his mind, and the flood of memories came rushing back.

James sat up abruptly, swinging his legs over the side of the bed. A sharp groan escaped him as the movement pulled at the still-healing wounds along his chest and back. His hands raked through his hair before trailing down to press against the fresh bandages on his torso.

"What happened." James turned his head slightly, locking onto Lia's deeply concerned gaze.

"What?" he whispered, feeling her concern seep into his very being.

Then, the earlier madness started again.

But this time, only Lia's emotions crashed through his shields in full stereo.

Fear.

Worry.

A confusing mesh of tangled feelings that threatened to wipe out his own sense of self.

Lia, deeply connected with James, observed him, waiting with the kind of patience that reassured him. He had only her emotions to contend with—but even then, others began to creep in, less intense yet still noticeable.

His new ability had a far longer range than hers.

Lia couldn't fathom having that much power. *No wonder he's having a difficult time.*

Difficult time? James projected through their link. *Try more like—hell,* he added, his struggle evident in the broadcasted words.

What is going on?

Lia stepped closer, extending her hands in a silent invitation. James reached out, linking them together.

The moment they touched, relief washed over him as the emotions and voices eased back.

James exhaled heavily. *Like a door closing,* he thought.

Lia nodded quickly. "Exactly," she agreed. "You need to find your own control—to close the door in your mind that blocks the emotions from overwhelming you."

James swallowed hard. "Why do they feel like a physical presence?" he asked, absorbing the stability of Lia's shields into himself.

Lia sat down on the bed, tilting her head toward the generous space between them. She smiled.

With their hands still clasped—neither wanting to lose the quiet in his mind—James eased closer, and they both turned toward each other. Their joined hands rested on his upper thighs.

"All emotions have energy. Depending on the strength of the emotion, the level or volume will vary. These feelings create physical reactions in our bodies that, for the most part, we ignore while experiencing them.

"As an empath, emotions react differently for me than they do for others. How each emotion's energy translates into a physical response in my brain may not be the same as how you experience it."

James started to open his mouth to speak.

Lia quickly shook her head, cutting him off. "I'm an empath. I've had this ability since I was eleven years old. When we... um, when we got..."

James tightened his grasp on her hands and gave them a gentle shake. "Out with it," he grumbled, feeling her apprehension like ants crawling across his brain.

Her nod was quick. She took in a deep breath and let it out before blurting, "When we became physically intimate, I think it accidentally merged us."

James frowned, shaking his head. "I've never heard of that happening before. My parents have special talents, but they've never shared theirs."

"I'm an empath, and apparently, I can link with my partner." Lia saw that James wanted to respond and quickly squeezed his hands to stop him. "Not just an intimate partner—like, a mate. A soulmate," she added softly.

James remained silent.

He had suspected something like this back in the jungle. However, this whole sharing of talent was a complication he hadn't anticipated. A prickling sensation spread in his mind, like static electricity coating the inside of his skull.

"What else?" James prompted.

He watched as Lia dropped her gaze from his.

"Lia?" he whispered. *What's happening, baby?* He directed the thought through their telepathic link.

She immediately looked back at him, her eyes betraying a vulnerability that tugged at his heart. Concern filled him—not for himself, only for her.

Letting out a soft sigh, Lia squared her shoulders. "Um... I—I kind of linked our life forces, too," she rushed out before blowing a burst of air from her lips.

"What?"

James' voice echoed in the room as he leapt from the bed, his body rigid with shock. His fingers raked through his hair—a clear sign of his growing agitation.

"Now everything falls into place," he muttered, his mind reeling from the implications of Lia's confession.

He **knew** his injuries that night had been life-threatening. He hadn't expected to survive and had been surprised each time he woke up afterward.

Was that because of Lia?

A cold sweat broke out on his forehead.

Good God She... she could have died because of me!

His panicked thoughts screamed through his mind, fear gripping his heart like a vice.

"I wouldn't have wanted to live if you had died," Lia said softly, her words a balm to his soul.

A wave of relief washed over him, easing the crushing weight of guilt from his shoulders.

But that didn't solve their current predicament, running rampant through her thoughts, *What were they going to do?*

Chapter Eleven

James began to move throughout the room, his mind a tumultuous sea of thoughts, much like the view outside the windows. He studied his surroundings, trying to shield his thoughts from her.

"You won't be able to do that right now," Lia said, her voice filled with concern. She stood up and headed toward the alcove overlooking the first floor below. The room abruptly ended with an open railing barrier facing the two-story window wall. Sitting on the bench nearby, she turned toward the spectacular view through the large windows.

The bay water appeared dark and choppy as the strong breeze pushed across its surface. Lia touched the railing with her fingers before turning back to watch James. The view from the alcove was breathtaking, with the dramatic swirling skyline in the distance and the sun casting a shimmering sheen on the water.

James was touching the book spines stacked within the built-in bookcase.

"In time, you'll learn control," Lia explained. "Just like with your other gifts. You'll be able to block even me out eventually."

James let out a loud grunt. "It's not that." He met Lia's steady gaze, spotting her pressed lips and raised eyebrows. He chuckled. "Okay, maybe that's part of it. I don't particularly appreciate sharing what I'm thinking all the time. Some thoughts are private."

"Agreed," Lia murmured, her voice heavy with guilt. A small smile appeared, only to quickly turn sad. "Do you hate me?" she asked, her shoulders drooping in defeat.

"No! No, Lia, baby. I love you," he admitted. "I'm worried sick about you!"

"Me...?" Lia shouted, jolting up from her seat. "I wasn't the one who purposely sacrificed himself to let his brothers and new lover escape!"

"Exactly!" James shouted back. "I did what I did so my brothers could live! I wanted them to get you out of there and be safe!"

"I didn't want to be safe if it put you in danger!" Lia's voice raised in volume to match his.

They both stood facing each other, with more than just the physical space of the room between them. This was their first hurdle, one that looked daunting and unsolvable, making all their previous predicaments seem like schoolyard drama.

With his posture stiff and jaw clenched, James wondered if he could still be as effective by doing things differently. His ability for rapid healing had served him well—even if he did push the limits sometimes, like with this last mission.

With her chin angled up and both hands fisted tightly against her thighs, Lia, a steadfast guardian, was resolute in her stance against James taking unnecessary risks.

Their harsh breathing, a testament to the tension in the room, was the only sound that filled the space.

Then, an old melody from a grandfather clock resonated from below. A series of repeating chimes marked the arrival of the top of the hour. James broke free from their staring contest and dragged his fingers roughly through his hair.

James' body could survive more damage than most. That was why he intercepted the small band of rebels who had managed to get a bead on their location while his brothers got Lia away.

Now that my life is tethered to Lia's— Not liking the direction of that particular thought, he shook his head, as if dispelling the unwanted notion, and swiftly eliminated the distance between them.

Lia watched as he approached, his bare-chested form a testament to his physical prowess, the pajama bottoms hanging low on his hips. His movements were fluid and powerful. *My warrior is back in spades,* that realization slipped out, causing her heartrate to increase.

"Yes, I am," he agreed, reaching for her hands. Unclenching them with his fingers, he brought them up to his lips. James transferred her hands into one of his, freeing his other hand to gently place on her face.

His palm softly cupped her cheek. "You are a gift that I never knew I wanted nor needed. How can I not want to protect that with everything I am?"

"I want to protect you, too," Lia replied. "We'll just have to find a way to meet in the middle."

"Compromise," James clarified while tugging her to him. "Compromise," he repeated softly into her sweet-smelling hair.

Lia mumbled something back, but it got lost in the contours of his hard chest.

Pushing her slightly away, James grinned. "What?"

"I said, why does it sound like you're trying to figure out a way around that word?" She brought her hands down to rest on her hips. "Because if you try, so will I."

James couldn't help the short laugh that escaped. "Okay. Point taken."

"Good," Lia returned. "Now, let's work on gaining control of your new ability."

James shrugged his shoulders, stretching his neck and back muscles. His injuries were still tight, another weakness that could keep him out of the fight. With a deep inhale followed by a long exhale, he responded, "Okay. But can you tell me what happened with Frank and my brothers first?"

Lia nodded, letting out a short burst of air. "Yup, but you won't like it," she promised.

"Not gonna lie, because you'd damn well know it anyway. But this whole situation—other than meeting you—has been one shit-storm after another."

"Agreed," Lia said softly, then leaned her body closer into his. She knew things were only going to get worse from here.

"It's not like the Commander betrayed his country or anything," Brian Patterson reasoned with the disgruntled group joining him.

Lia let her attention stray outside through the two-story windows. Combative voices and overlapping opinions dominated the downstairs living room—even if most were there via Skype.

She hadn't even had the chance to talk to her mother to find out if Michelle Robinson knew about Frank Marshall's fabricated history. Knowing it was for protection from unseen and unknown possible enemies her father might have had, Lia was engulfed in a whirlwind of doubts, feeling like her whole life had been a big lie.

And it didn't work. Lia mused. *This past week's abduction happened anyway.*

Signaling to his brothers, James slowly shook his head toward the viewing device a few times before easing his arm around Lia, a gesture of unwavering support that reassured her.

Lia turned back, sending him a small smile before worry settled back on her expression.

"Guys, we need to concentrate on the present and let the past go for right now. Once we have a game plan and Lia's no longer a target, we can debate why he did it," James inserted into the mix, emphasizing the group's unity and shared goal.

Reaching for James' hand, Lia pulled it onto her lap. The physical contact helped her stay focused, so she tightened her hold around his.

James' hand gently squeezed back. His lips grazed her forehead before turning to face his brothers on the large-screen television—that also functioned as a computer monitor.

Apparently, this hide-a-hole had the latest technology, with a fast internet connection to a compact server. The clarity of the picture was just like having his brothers in the room. *Though it's not quite the same thing.*

But James realized this method worked better.

At least until his lack of control over absorbing all their Alpha-like, high-powered emotions didn't result in a stroke—especially with them all hyped up about Lia's situation and their equally challenging life forces, now intertwined, causing their concerns.

"We will find out the extent of Marshall's deception after this is over," James repeated, promising them with his determined expression that they would get the answers they sought. "Sean, I need eyes on Herrera at all times. Can we put a tracking device on his phone?"

"Workin' on it," Sean responded, bringing a handheld electrical device into view of the video camera.

James watched as Sean brought up a command prompt onto their wall-mounted monitor screen linked to his phone. The screen smoothly divided between all their separate video-conferencing windows and the computer program.

"As soon as Herrera clicks on the text message from a UN clerk assistant I've sent him, I can clone his account. Plus, one of our independent contacts owes me a favor. He's ready to move into position once I give him the green light." Sean divided his attention between the many computer hacks on multiple monitors he was currently working on and the Skype conference he was hosting between all of them.

James edged further off the sofa, rocking his weight forward as if a call to action would go down at any moment.

Lia understood his impatience. Ever since he regained consciousness, the sweep of adrenaline had washed over him like waves crashing onto the shore. She just needed him to calm down so they could concentrate on handling his new ability.

The silent questions itched louder than she'd admit.

Did he understand covert missions were a no-go until he could function around people?

And more importantly, would James be able to sit this one out while his brothers remained in harm's way?

Chapter Twelve

J ames turned to Lia and gave another shake of his head. Their internal link clued him in on her train of thought. "I get that, love," James declared with a heavy, full exhale of air.

"Get what?" Josh piqued in on the screen.

"I've got to figure out control so I can get the hell out of here and help you guys," James grumbled back.

"Chill, bro," Josh teased before quickly dropping the playful demeanor. His facial expression turned severe, and his attention switched to Brian, who stood beside him, before returning to the screen. Josh's and Brian's stances and expressions mirrored each other.

Sean's expression was similar, too.

James didn't need his newfangled gift to pick up what they were all dishing out.

"We're of one mind that you staying put is for the best right now," Sean disclosed in a soft, measured tone that might have seemed deceptive if you didn't know him.

But that wasn't the case with James; he knew Sean well. Leaping up, James launched into a parade of curses and threats, knowing what was coming next.

"Orders came down from Marshall. You stay on medical leave until he says otherwise," Sean said over James's tirade.

Lia understood James's need to rant. Knowing this tension required release made sense. She knew getting sidelined like this didn't sit well with the type of man James and his brothers were. The need to protect others and fight the evils in this world was hardwired into their DNA.

Her attention returned to the TV screen and locked onto the Patterson brothers' gazes. She carefully nodded once and watched as they confirmed that they had seen her message loud and clear.

They stood unified in this decision.

James would stay put, even if she had to knock him out to keep him out of the fight. Conveniently enough, the eight small, 23-gauge x 1-inch precision glide intramuscular needles given to her by Frank Marshall would help do the trick.

James leaving beforehand would be an exercise in what not to do. He would be a significant liability, with his overloaded emotions quickly taking him under, leaving him vulnerable to attack—or worse.

Everyone on the team had been brought up to speed on the consequences of either James or Lia's demise. The expression, 'one stone in hand getting two birds in the bush,' had never seemed more real.

James continued pacing in front of the sitting arrangement. His inability to charge into action left him spinning like a kite in the wind.

Where is my legendary control?

Down the freaking toilet, that's where, James argued with himself.

Clearing her throat softly, Lia brought James's attention back onto the screen.

The oldest Patterson brother swiftly refocused his mind and began shouting out orders. "Josh, I'll need you to work with Sean on figuring out the ties to Suavez's hired muscle in the U.S. If they still have the contract on Lia, I want to know what direction it will most likely come from."

James turned slightly and let his intense gaze rest on Lia.

She sat back into the full depths of the cushions with her feet tucked under her. James's mind churned, quickly connecting some possible outcomes. Aware of his thoughts, she didn't need the scowl forming on his face to know he wasn't pleased with any of them—especially since he wouldn't be out there with his brothers, helping.

"You're no good to them right now," Lia said in a calm, clear voice.

James's brothers stayed silent. Instead, their eyes bounced back and forth from James to Lia. They suspected an internal conversation was happening before them.

They were correct.

Lia went through James's list and blew holes in every option.

James, knowing she was correct, only added to his frustration.

"What would you have me do?" James rumbled out loud, raising his hands before settling them on his hips.

"Stay here, gain some control of the empathic ability, and let your brothers do the heavy lifting. For right now, anyway. You can provide strategic support and coordination," Lia relayed with sharp precision.

She caught Josh's quick grin on the screen before he changed it to a calm, neutral expression.

"Bro, Lia's right. You need to sit this one out. Provide security for Lia and yourself," Sean added, his voice steady. He had turned his body away from them off-screen.

James looked up and watched as Josh and Brian nodded in agreement.

Letting out a heavy sigh, James nodded once in capitulation. He strode swiftly back to the sofa and swept Lia into his arms. He plopped down onto the cushions with her on his lap. His gaze turned toward his brothers. "I'll stay here while I work on handling being around people."

"Well, since you already suck at being around people, there can only be improvement with Lia's help," Josh ribbed him.

James lifted one hand off Lia's hip to shoot his middle finger toward his brother—which only made Josh salute him back in kind.

"Okay, then let's leave it with this: Brian coordinates with Marshall on what the agency will officially sanction. Sean, get information on Herrera and Suavez's power organizational chart. I want to know who all the players are and where they're presently located. Get Josh to help. Let me know what strings to pull myself. I'm not you, but I'm better than most."

James rested his chin on top of Lia's head and took in a big whiff of her hibiscus-smelling shampoo.

Lia was astonished at how quickly James shored up avenues and strategic counterpoints. His mind worked exceptionally fast.

James' grip around her waist tightened. He spun her around so that their fronts came together. "We'll work on control of this empathic power this afternoon and then try it out. Does this hideaway have a town or something?"

"Something," Lia answered with a grin and added, "Not much of one."

"Good. We will start slow and make our way from there. I'll need to prepare myself in case my brothers need backup."

"We won't," all James' brothers shouted in unison.

James shifted Lia to the side so he could look up at them. "You never know. You might," he replied, a grin spreading across his face. Gathering Lia tight to his chest, James lowered his head, allowing his mouth to reach her ear. "They can't do much without me." His voice held a smug attitude that came naturally.

Lia should have found it annoying, but she didn't.

James smirked and bit her lobe lightly. "Oh, I know already. I felt that shiver of desire loud and clear."

Lia pushed off his chest to get some separation between their bodies, but James didn't allow her an inch. She arched her back so her eyes could meet his. "Can you feel my annoyance right now?" she grumbled.

James just laughed. "No, all I feel is that you want me. Very, very badly."

Lia tried to keep a straight face, but the laugh won out. "God, you're so full of yourself."

James just shook his head, his face holding a determined glare. "If you keep sending me all those vibes of desperately wanting me, I'm not going to be the only one full of me."

Lia swiftly turned and brought her attention back to the large-screen TV. She saw a wide grin spread across each of James' brothers' faces. Josh even tried not to laugh but quickly failed.

Lia glared at them before turning to James, equally annoyed. "You better watch yourself," she threatened softly.

"Oh, come on, you two," Josh groaned in pain. "Keep the foreplay to when you're alone. I don't think we can keep from gagging with both of your goo-goo eyes shooting back and forth."

Brian, keeping a serious facial expression, chimed in, "If that's all the orders, bro, we're going to sign off. We'll sync up in a few hours."

Josh pushed Brian out of the way to shut down the video connection. "So please try to get it out of your systems by then. If the big super-soldier stays behind, I need my food to stay down to keep my energy levels up."

"Well, good luck with that, bro," Sean joked. "I have a sneaky suspicion they won't get this out of their systems for years to come."

"You got that right," James agreed.

Lia swatted his arm and glared up at him with squinty eyes. "I don't know... It seems more like minutes to me."

"Liar," James growled softly into her ear.

Lia shivered and sighed softly. "Yeah... liar," she confirmed while combing her fingers through his unruly hair. It felt so soft in her hands. She drew his head down, wanting his lips on hers.

When their lips joined, Lia immediately felt the powerful pull. Heat quickly encapsulated her mind and body. Her body sank into his hardness as she surrendered to the feelings overtaking her senses.

James quickly turned; a grimace stole across his lips before it vanished. He only cared about one thing at the moment while laying Lia down on the sofa's cushions. Shifting his weight allowed him to lean between her legs. He briefly heard chuckles coming from the peanut gallery before they severed the video link.

Thankful for some privacy, James couldn't stop himself from following Lia down to the cushions to save his life. To him, being with this woman saved him from a fate worse than death. He felt so much—so alive when he was with her. He knew she was his salvation.

His mouth sought to taste her. The need to know every flavor, every sensitive pulse point she owned, and the feel of her delicate skin drove him onward. His lips skimmed along her collarbone.

Lia tilted her head back, giving him more access. She moaned when his tongue stroked a path along her skin.

Suddenly, James stiffened. He eased back and turned his head to the side.

Lia opened her eyes and aimed her attention at what pulled him away.

A gasp quickly sprung out from her wet, glistening lips.

The furniture surrounding them—including the sofa they lay upon—floated in the air a few inches off the floor.

"THAT isn't my doing," James clarified while studying Lia closely.

Quickly afterward, the furniture instantly plopped back down to the floor with multiple sounding thuds.

"Ah," Lia said softly in disbelief. "I guess we swapped more than just my empathic ability."

Chapter Thirteen

A few hours later, James was sweaty and tired.

Unfortunately, his present condition wasn't related to the activity he had hoped for. There was a slight snafu with furniture moving every time their passions exceeded past heavy petting. So, they had to halt their lovemaking until James found a way around that minor problem.

Instead, he and Lia were working on building a solid shield around his new empathic ability. However, keeping the barrier stable in his mind proved harder than anticipated.

They discovered that when he stayed in close physical proximity to Lia, it was doable, but the instant they separated for any significant distance, problems arose. His barrier became flimsy at best.

With a frustrated exhale, James hurried back inside. The slamming of the front door easily conveyed his emotional turmoil.

Lia waited in the den, which also served as a guest bedroom. She turned away from the large glass window facing the front yard, where she had been maintaining visual contact while James drove the old, banged-up Chevy pickup truck further down the dirt road past the edge of the house's property line. They had tested the distance of proximity and determined how far they could separate before Lia couldn't assist James with his shields. Her commitment to James' struggle was unwavering, but they certainly had opposing objectives—her approach leaned more on the rational side, understanding their limited time constraints.

James stomped up the stairs, his determination echoing in each step. Deep shadows under his eyes showed the exhaustion settling in, but he remained adamant about mastering this new ability in one day. His stubbornness knew no bounds.

"I can do better than this," he said while puffing out of breath.

"You're recovering from multiple bullet wounds, James. Rome wasn't built in a day," Lia reasoned, knowing his need for an instant fix clashed with the reality of the process caused his frustrations.. Tilting her head back and rolling it slowly from side to side, she was beyond tired herself—and she hadn't been shot like him.

It was a test of her resilience to extend a protection barrier around James' newly formed shield while also keeping a tight hold on this new telekinesis ability. The broken lamp, picture frame, and numerous coffee mugs were evidence of her struggle.

But her perseverance to master it weighed on her fiercely—for James' sake.

James hesitated—something inconsistent with his usual confidence—before pulling her into his arms. "I'm sorry, love. I know I'm pushing us both past our endurance, but I have a terrible suspicion we won't have much time before trouble finds us. I need to be able to handle myself, or I'm no good to you." His voice, coated with fear, revealed a side of him Lia rarely saw.

Lia held tight to his upper arms. "I know, but there's a middle ground between doing nothing and pushing yourself too much, too soon. You need to give yourself a day or two. We have some time to spare, don't we?" She looked up and met his gaze.

James studied her for a few seconds, then nodded. He let his chin rest on the top of her head, breathing in her tantalizing scent and taking a moment to enjoy their embrace.

Lia tucked her face into his chest. His rich, musky, almost smoky pine scent reminded her of walking in the woods at night.

"Are you sniffing me?" James chuckled.

"Yup," she admitted. "I love the way you smell." She pressed her face deeper into his shirt and took a deep inhale.

James' chest rumbled with laughter, instantly becoming Lia's new favorite sound. Until now, she hadn't heard him laugh much, and she could hardly blame him after the week they'd had. But she hoped all that would change in the foreseeable future. She longed to hear more of that deep, timbering, sexy sound that brought warmth and joy to their relationship.

"I'm hungry," she announced. "Let's go into town and see how you do. We'll get something to eat, test your control, and then come back here for a break. You can work on whatever your brothers send you, and maybe we can watch a movie together afterward."

Lia looked up and smiled. "Sound like a plan?" she asked, gauging his reaction.

James took another deep inhale of her and nodded slowly. "Let me call Frank first and get an update from him. Then we'll head out," he replied, pulling her closer. He couldn't seem to find the need for space. The more time they spent together, the more he craved this physical contact. As the perpetual Lone Wolf of his family, that should have freaked him out—but it didn't.

Instead, James had never felt more at ease in his whole life, as if he had found a missing piece of himself.

"Me too," Lia whispered. Then quickly added, "Sorry, but you're practically shouting that thought at me." She giggled, her playful nature adding a lightness to his life that he sorely needed.

James shook his head, a wide grin spreading across his face. "Damn, I have to find some control. I don't want to keep projecting sappy thoughts at you. I mean, I have a reputation as a hard-ass to maintain."

"Don't worry," Lia responded, punching him in the arm. "I won't lose my head or anything," she grumbled.

"But I *want* you to," James teased back. "I want you to lose your head and heart just like I did for you."

"Aww... there you go with being a hard ass again," Lia joked, smirking mischievously. But inside her heart she beamed with happiness. James had nothing to worry about on that account. Her heart and head became lost the moment their eyes had met, and with their tethered connection, James could feel it.

The small town of Milfred, Delaware, exuded a unique charm, blending a backwoods persona with a seashore vibe. Nestled by the Delaware Bay, the resident population hovered around seventy-six, but during peak seasons, the town came alive with over a hundred visitors, adding a dynamic twist to its serene atmosphere.

It was close to November, and tourism was a distant memory, leaving the locals to enjoy the slower traffic.

Pushing open the large, wood-paneled door, James tucked Lia close to his side while stepping into the Milfred General

Store, which appeared to serve as both a grocery and hardware store.

It was all too wide open for James to feel comfortable. With nowhere to hide and unfamiliar townspeople around, there were too many unknown variables to work out. So far, he had noticed six people in their immediate vicinity, three of whom appeared to be employees.

Keeping Lia's hand in his, James opened his mind and scanned the surrounding area. He lowered his newly constructed shields slowly, allowing emotions to filter into his mind. The nearby ones poured in like water through an opened dam.

Although the clerk smiled brightly, James immediately felt a prickling, scratching sensation on his brain that told him another story. The young woman, wearing a quizzical expression, turned toward Lia.

With their telepathic link wide open, Lia and James were in perfect sync, experiencing the world around them as one. This unique bond not only connected them on a deeper level but also allowed them to navigate their surroundings with a shared understanding.

"She's nervous about something," James said softly. Stopping his forward movement, he organized the jumbled thoughts and emotions streaming through him. "She's nervous because the guy she likes is working with her today."

James pointed to the clerk, who was diligently stocking the shelves. "He's nursing a silent crush on her, but he's convinced she doesn't feel the same way." A shiver ran down James's spine, and he winced. "And that woman over there," he nodded toward a young shopper, "she's feeling a surge of desire towards me."

Lia chuckled at his reaction. She leaned closer into James' body, sending the married shopper a warning look. Although, Lia really couldn't blame her. James did look very sexy in faded jeans and a form-fitting t-shirt that showed off his muscles.

He rolled his eyes and sighed loudly. With Lia in his arms, he shifted away, severing Lia's staring contest with the other woman. He put a slight squeeze in his hold and quickly kissed the top of Lia's head. "Someone in the back is annoyed with the two clerks and wants them to quit with the drama and get to work. Also, someone else is frustrated about whose turn it is to pick up the kids from daycare."

James spun around again and looked to his right. "I feel a lightness and a warmth around my mind." James turned back to face Lia. "But I don't know where it's coming from or its context."

Lia nodded and closed her eyes, pushing her abilities further out. After a few moments, she smiled and turned toward James. "Your range is incredible. You're catching someone not in the store. Someone is in the next parking lot over at the Mispillion River Brewing Company. A customer in their parking lot is laughing."

"How do you know it's female versus male?" James asked.

"Female emotions are mostly... Ah, I guess it's lighter than the male counterpart. Except when extreme dark emotions are at play—then there is no comparison between males and females. You'll feel and pick up on the differences real quick."

"Okay," James replied, then grinned. "I'm ready to try it on my own."

Lia shook her head from side to side. "There are too many people, James. It will be too much."

James pulled his hand away. "Go a few aisles away; let me try on my own. Oh, and don't throw anything around with your telekinesis."

Lia sighed heavily, shaking her head at his stubbornness, and did as he ordered.

"Ordered... is a little bit strong," James said while walking away. "I'd say strongly suggested."

Snorting loudly, Lia quickly grabbed a handbasket and continued moving further away. She only hoped she would be more successful at controlling her new power than she had been earlier today.

Without the physical boundaries tethering James to Lia, the emotions quickly bombarded him. He felt like a small boat rocking and sweeping along on a large body of water during a storm. His heart raced, his breath quickened, and sweat quickly dotted his temples and upper lip.

James concentrated on letting the energy flow around him, not allowing it to get absorbed into his mind. Lia had described the exercise as turning the weight of the emotions into the equivalent of a giant bubble, each separately encapsulated and floating above him, just out of reach.

His body began to shake with the energy he was expending to handle the stimulation overload—from just this small group. James had mistakenly thought that since they all seemed mild-mannered in appearance, he'd be able to handle their light emotions.

Oh man, was I wrong, James reprimanded himself. *How does Lia take this every day?*

"I didn't handle it all at once," Lia said, coming up from behind him. Her hand grabbed his, and the swirling chaos in his head immediately quieted down a few notches.

James gripped her hand tightly, his frustration palpable. "I'm never going to get the hang of this," he grumbled, but his resolve remained unwavering. To protect Lia, he had to master this.

"Yes, you are," Lia insisted, her voice a soothing balm. "Just not in a day," she added, her patience a comforting presence even as she kept in a gasp of discomfort. James, too overwhelmed with the chaos in his mind, didn't realize the power of his grip.

"Now, let's finish shopping," Lia insisted, her guidance a steadying anchor. "Using me as a slight buffer, separate each emotion in your head. Remember to put them in a floating bubble to keep them from overloading you." She led him down the nearest aisle, even though she didn't like the look of James' complexion; his face had lost color.

But at least he remains conscious with no nosebleeds. That is an improvement, Lia thought. Taking it as a positive step forward made her feel better, but she couldn't shake the worry that if James didn't learn to control his powers, it could lead to more serious consequences.

"Barely," James grumbled back, a heavy sense of responsibility weighing on him, fully aware of what was at stake.

"We'll take it," Lia replied, her actions casual while gesturing with her chin toward a display of olives. "We need some of those and some French bread." She continued down a few aisles, her movements purposely relaxed as she dropped an assortment of items into her basket.

James watched as the few customers shopped nearby. It was hard to believe that their casual indifference hid a cauldron of heavy emotions.

"Great, as if people weren't already an immense pain in my ass," James muttered to himself.

He heard a slight chuckle in his mind and felt a warmth of brightness surrounding his thoughts and heart. It humbled him. Never believing he deserved this, he remained in awe of the gift—a mysterious juncture that had saved him from the brink of what Frank Marshall swore could be worse than death itself.

The loss of one's humanity could result in all sorts of calamities to the spirit.

James wouldn't let a day go by without extending gratitude to his Maker for this wonderful miracle. And with another prayer following suit directly afterward, he hoped he had whatever it took to keep Lia from harm.

Because he knew danger could be at their doorstep before they knew it.

Chapter Fourteen

Two hours later, James struggled to stay awake now that he had eaten that big meal. All his body wanted to do was rest.

But I have too much to do! James reminded himself and fought hard against the sleepiness.

"Yeah, like properly recovering from almost dying a few days ago," Lia muttered, her patience wearing thin after witnessing how much he continued to push himself. Clearing away the dirty dishes from dinner, she attempted to rein in her frustration.

The buzzing of the communication device in the living room couldn't have come at a better time, sparing James from getting a swift kick in the rear from Lia.

James hurried to the adjacent room. His new empathic ability wasn't necessary to know Lia's patience had reached its limit. Typing in a few keystrokes on the tablet, he activated the monitor screen, and Frank Marshall's face appeared.

"You look like shit," Frank quickly said. "I'll make this quick."

James huffed out a nonverbal reply and leaned against the nearby desk.

"Sit yourself the hell down," Frank ordered.

"How's my mother?" Lia asked, coming out from the kitchen and tugging James toward the sofa.

"In a secure location." Frank shrugged his shoulders up and down to relieve some muscle tension. He held up a small device displaying what appeared to be a security feed. Lia spotted her mother in the video. Michelle Robinson seemed comfortable, moving around at ease in the small cottage Frank had assigned for security and safety reasons.

Frank waited a moment to let Lia take in the sight before adding, "She's impatient to talk to you, but I can't let that happen for a while. We must ensure no one is scouting around her to get to you."

Lia nodded in understanding before shifting her attention to James, who had fallen fast asleep, his head resting against the sofa's back cushions. His breathing remained deep and steady.

Lia returned to the monitor screen, sighing. Shrugging her shoulders, she admitted, "I knew as soon as I got him to remain still for more than a minute, this would happen. He is pushing himself way too hard."

Frank Marshall studied James. He had witnessed this man's rise in ranks within the department until Patterson started blocking any promotion that would take him out of combat. But Frank hadn't exaggerated earlier when assessing James' condition. Noting the lack of color in his complexion and the deep shadows under his eyes, Frank released a heavy sigh.

Switching his attention back to Lia, he said, "He can handle pushing himself, Lia. Don't be too hard on him for doing what needs doing."

With Lia's patience at its lowest, that wasn't what she wanted to hear. Adding to her frustration was the revelation that her entire life had been a lie, orchestrated by her godfather. It made it extremely easy to snap.

She blasted him, "Frank, you don't get to tell me what I can and can't do. Not right now. And not like this. I'm inside his head. I can see what no one else can see. He came very close to dying. He needs to give his body a chance to bounce back naturally before making demands from it again."

"Maybe," Frank admitted before looking away. He adjusted something on his desk that wasn't visible in the video feed. Clearing his throat softly, he shifted in his chair before refocusing on Lia. "I'm not going to stop trying to take care of the people I love. Even if they're mad at me."

"I'm not mad... exactly," Lia said stiffly before allowing the rest to rush out. "I just need to be sure about some things."

"Be sure that your well-being and that of the man beside you are my only concern now. I know more than most what I'm asking from both of you." Frank spoke in an even, low tone, but Lia, knowing him well, heard the deep emotions in his voice.

She nodded in understanding. Her emotions were still unresolved from everything that went down the past few days, but she knew the caliber of man he strove to be. "Do you want me to have James call you when he wakes up?" she asked instead.

Frank sighed heavily once more. Knowing that keeping secrets exacted a hefty price, he let it go. "No, I will be unavailable for the next day or two." He paused briefly, his gaze directed away from the camera as a few moments of silence stretched between them.

When his gaze returned to the screen, he added, "Tell James I'll call him back then, and until that time, I ordered him to take some time off and get some rest. Things here will keep."

Frank jerked his chin down once before continuing, "And Lia, if you believe he's not ready and he tries to join up with his brothers, do what I told you to and keep him under as long as possible. I know what I'm asking and the cost you might pay. But his life is worth the sacrifice." With quick, sure movements, he reached up and disconnected their communication.

Lia let her shoulders relax into the cushions and blew her breath out slowly. Turning slightly, she watched James sleeping.

Standing up carefully to avoid jostling the cushions, she spread a soft afghan across his upper body. Heading out of the room, she sighed, not liking where her thoughts went.

Can I take James' freedom of choice away? Even if it saves our lives?

Chapter Fifteen

An hour and a half later, James thrashed in his sleep. A dream about escaping the drug cartel had its grip on him and wouldn't let go. Almost a week had passed since Lia and he had raced through the Mexican jungle, but his mind played the memory out like watching it on a movie theater screen:

The vividly heart-shaped green leaves slapped against James' hand as he pushed them away. Shifting his body to block the palms from approaching further, he allowed Lia to follow through a slim opening into the small clearing.

James paused his brutal pace to hand Lia a canteen.

As she grabbed it, James tightened his hold and waited until Lia's gaze met his. "Just take a sip," he instructed.

After the unexpected killing of Raul Ortego, Lia and James found themselves in a perilous escape from the rebels' encampment. The inconvenient timing of the day, the scorching heat, and the demanding pace all added to the danger. James, driven by an overpowering need to keep Lia safe, pushed them even harder.

Lia nodded and quickly went for the water again. When their fingers came into contact, physical awareness traveled up from Lia's hand, making her whole body tingle. She took the canteen and stumbled back. Quickly turning away from him, she did as instructed and sipped water. But she really wanted to guzzle the whole thing down to cool off the temperature in both her body and libido.

He stepped back, creating more distance between them. Their attraction had ignited before, but each time their physical contact sparked, it seemed to intensify.

Both James and Lia fought against the relentless pull of their desires. James had a feeling that this internal battle would reach a breaking point sooner rather than later.

James figured the faster they met up with the rest of his gang, the faster they would have a deterrent.

It wasn't enough that they were in a bug-infested, snake-crawling jungle, with a band of bad guys pursuing them. The heat between them and the pull to do something about their attraction was that much stronger.

The water canteen was pushed into his back, giving him the prod to get his priorities under wraps. James quickly turned around and stored the canteen back in his knapsack—the same one he'd stashed outside the rebel camp two days before.

"We need to keep moving," James said softly. "Can you keep this pace up for another hour or two?"

Lia just nodded and repositioned the smaller bag on her shoulder. It resembled a toddler's school backpack compared to his size, but it still felt like she was carrying a load of rocks for days.

James hesitated briefly, his mouth opened, then quickly shut again. He shook his head once and started to move away.

Lia knew enough to leave it alone, but she didn't.

Call it the devil whispering in her ear.Call it being too tired to think straight. But she did as the voice prompted. She stopped his forward movement by grabbing his arm as he went to pass her. "What were you going to say?" she asked.

He just shook his head once again and moved to go around her.

Lia, letting that coaxing whisper take over, blocked him and got her body into his personal space. "What. Were. You. Going. To. Say!" she demanded this time, poking her finger in his chest.

"I don't think you want to do that," James warned.

Lia defiantly angled her chin. "Maybe I do."

"Careful, Lia," James warned again. He broke eye contact with her and quickly scanned the surrounding area.

They hadn't heard anyone following them in a few hours, but James had hoped to gain a little more buffer between them and the ragtag team of soldiers-for-hire tailing them.

"James," Lia said softly, barely there.

But her voice ran through James' head like a battering ram. He had only a slim band left of control around his desire. Just looking at her strained his resolve.

The shirt James had given Lia earlier was swimming on her small frame. The open neckline fell to one side, exposing the creamy softness of her skin, reminding him of butterscotch candy.

Having sensed how far gone he quickly became, Lia decided to tip the scales further. She stepped closer. Her nipples beaded into hard points against James' chest, branding him through the light covering of his T-shirt.

James' control broke with a muttered curse. He tore away her backpack and threw it to the ground. His bag went next. Pulling her tight to his chest, he lowered his lips to hers.

When they kissed, their attraction flared red-hot. The passion they both tried to ignore overtook them in a roaring explosion of want. They both moaned with need.

The need to drive further into this onslaught of sensations rose.

The need to be consumed by this burning obsession took over.

Lia quickly unbuttoned his shirt and dove through the gap she made to touch his skin. His chest held a hardness and strength that beckoned her to mold and explore.

James pulled at her shirt and wrestled it over her head. Breaking their embrace for a short moment, he quickly removed his shirt.

They both dived back into each other's arms as soon as the clothes on their upper bodies were gone.

His mouth sucked and tasted the warm, salty skin on her neck and throat.

Lia moaned, her neck losing the strength to keep her head upright. She swiftly surrendered to the weakness and allowed her head to drop back.

Another moan and shiver escaped when James took advantage of having more access to her. He lightly bit and licked along a path to her collarbone. "Lia, I want you so much," James admitted in a rough growl.

"Want you," Lia moaned back.

Suddenly, James pushed them forward until a wide tree trunk prevented them from moving any further.

James quickly unfastened the khaki pants—another article of clothing he had supplied for her earlier. A growl of frustration soon followed when his makeshift rope rigging for a belt prevented his access.

The jungle's heat, humidity, and sweat from a fast-paced journey soaked into the fiber and tightened the knots, making it impossible to loosen.

James reached for his pocketknife and began sawing through the rope with quick, controlled movements.

Lia watched in total fascination as the strength in his arm flexed with every jerk of the knife. She should have been concerned with the sharp edges and the proximity to her flesh, but she wasn't.

All she cared about was losing her pants.

James chuckled. The connection of their telepathic link allowed him to hear her eagerness to destroy the innocent rope.

"Almost," he promised, and soon afterward, the pants dropped with the tearing of the rope's fibers.

Lia stepped quickly out of the encumbering clothing. The obsession with being joined by this man was all she could think about.

Picking her up, James brought her legs around his waist and pressed her back against the tree bark. His head bent forward, and his lips enveloped her berry-colored nipple in his mouth.

Lia tightened her legs around his middle, pulling him even closer toward her. She growled when her hot, moist core rubbed against his rock-hard member.

"James!" Lia commanded as her upper body arched in response to the sucking pull on her breasts. It was as if a direct nerve ending

connected her breast to her sweet spot. The intense pleasure ripped an orgasm out of her.

James lowered his briefs and freed his member.

Lia's head rolled from side to side against the tree trunk. "James," she implored.

Suddenly, the dream dissolved away as sleep abruptly turned to wakefulness.

Chapter Sixteen

J ames shot up in bed, moaning loudly as his dream cascaded into reality, an exploding sensory overload crashing through him.

A naked Lia straddled James' hips, rocking her wet core against him.

She positioned his heavy erection at the entrance of her feminine opening.

James let out a loud hiss of intense pleasure, sinking into the fiery wet glove that barely took all of him. Lia rocked on him, her eyes closed in intense pleasure as her teeth lightly bit her lower lip.

"Lia!" James shouted. The ricocheting waves of shared pleasure sent waves of sensations coursing through him. His hips pistoned with rough and powerful strokes. The need to reach that pinnacle obliterated his finesse and control.

James' guttural cry escaped as Lia's inner muscles pulsed tightly around his virile member. The explosion of his release bordered on pain—so intense was the pleasure.

The empathic bond added another dimension to their relationship he hadn't counted on. Sharing pleasure like this brought intimacy like this to a whole new level he had never experienced before. His heartbeat throbbed so hard it felt like it was moving his ribcage, cracking it wide open.

Lia slumped onto his chest, breathing rapidly from their physical exertion. Her lips licked the salty moisture coating James' skin. She enjoyed feeling his large frame shudder from her touch.

James' eyes remained closed as his body recovered. If their lovemaking got any better, James didn't think he'd survive it.

But boy, oh boy, what a way to go, his musings countered.

Grinning against James' chest hair, Lia's fingers moved from his hips to press against his breastbone. "It's not beating too hard," she said while patting his skin. "You'll be alright in a minute."

James snagged her down and turned them both onto their sides. His gaze finally focused on their surroundings.

Lia had moved the guest room's futon mattresses into the living room. James slightly leaned up and looked around.

Somebody had been busy. The sofa, tables, and lamps had been moved out of the room. Craning his neck, James could just make out the pieces piled together in the adjacent dining room.

James grinned and turned back toward Lia.

Lia had a big smile spread across her face. "Well, Rip Van Winkle, I had some time while you snored. Seemed like a good solution to a problem we were having."

"Yup," he said while tenderly tucking a strand of hair behind her ear. He bent down and kissed her, and within one heartbeat to the next, their growing need for each other flashed back to life.

"What do you mean he went to intercept?" James sat up on the mattress and grimaced. His injuries were rapidly healing, but his muscles still protested with any sharp movement.

"Sean got confirmation from a trusted source that Suarez landed at Gerald's Airport, just south of the Virginia state border. He left a few hours ago to lead a small team to shadow and, if possible, apprehend the target," Brian reported. His image on screen had his game face on.

Knowing the oldest Patterson as he did, Brian anticipated the following response. He was always ready to shut down whatever cockamamie plan James was about to spout off, a dynamic that had developed over years of working together.

James carefully donned his t-shirt and glanced at Lia as she lay asleep just inches away from him. Carefully leaving the mattress, he headed out of the room toward the kitchen. Getting a mug full of coffee sounded imperative right now.

He and Lia had a day and last night to themselves before the outside world burst the bubble they had been living in. James was surprised they had that long before the mission—one of utmost importance—imploded upon their slight reprieve.

However short, they both needed that time to recharge. Especially James. And his body felt stronger for it, too.

"Send a small team to the safe house to protect Lia. I'll be there as soon as the helicopter can pick me up," James ordered, his voice filled with a protective urgency.

"No team." Josh popped his head into the camera's sightline. "You are staying put. We have this, Commander." Josh's customary casualness was gone, replaced with a deadly intensity that reflected through the video.

James slammed the upper cabinet door closed after retrieving a black ceramic mug. Only three were left of an eight-piece set after Lia's mini-practicing exercise the other day.

The glass in the wood-framed door still rattled from James' forceful treatment. "You don't get to make that call," James said softly into his phone.

"You are correct, Commander," Josh said back just as softly. "These orders came down from above. I'm just following them."

James swore with tightly suppressed fury, his knuckles turning white as he gripped the phone. "Like hell. We'll see. One call to Marshall will fix that."

Josh whipped his gaze toward Brian.

In turn, Brian looked away briefly, raised his arms, and folded them across his chest with his hands tucked under his armpits. He glared at the video chat camera. "Orders from Marshall are clear. You are to stay with Lia until he personally contacts you and says otherwise. You can try contacting him yourself, but we can't reach him at this time."

"Well then, I'll go against orders." James propped his phone up along the counter's backsplash. He grabbed his laptop and began searching for transportation options.

"Stand down, Commander," Brian said with quiet authority. "This is not your battle. You have your orders."

"I'll make some calls and see about that," James repeated. His forefinger pressed the red circle on his cell phone, deactivating the video call.

He watched as the Keurig coffee maker dispensed the dark fluid into his cup. As he turned toward the container of sugar, he spotted Lia leaning against the cased door opening nearby.

She stood dressed in one of his cotton shirts, a reminder of their shared intimacy. The dark blue fabric stopped just above her knees. As his eyes traveled from the hem down to her smooth, tan legs and feet. He noticed the slight pink shade of her nail-polished toes.

James stopped abruptly and met her wary gaze.

Lia pushed off the door trim, went to the refrigerator, and opened the door. With her back toward James, she blankly viewed the items before her, concentrating on keeping her panic hidden and formulating a plan to keep James from rushing into battle.

A heavy silence reigned between them for several moments. When Lia continued to peer inside the appliance, James reached around her and snatched the heavy cream.

"Let me help you with that," James said, gently guiding Lia out of the door swing's path and shutting the door carefully. He poured cream into the coffee mug, added a small amount of sugar, and handed the hot beverage to Lia.

Reaching up to the cabinet beside her, he got another mug down for himself.

Lia took a sip of her coffee—done precisely to her liking. She raised her gaze to watch James as he retrieved a new coffee pod from the bamboo, storage kiosk alongside the coffee maker and placed it into the machine.

James pushed the button to brew another cup and turned around to meet her penetrating gaze.

"I'm going to go get a shower," Lia calmly stated before walking out.

Chapter Seventeen

"**S**hit," James exclaimed while watching Lia's retreating form.

He began to follow her but suddenly stopped. "Fuck!" he cursed softly, torn between two decisions.

Turning back, he picked up his laptop and searched for small-plane airstrips near him. He also quickly accessed the multiple pieces of information Josh and Brian had sent him and started formulating other options.

There was no time like the present to start doing things differently.

If James couldn't be there for his brothers in person, he would damn well be planning some strategic and intelligence counter-support for whatever shit would hit the fan.

With a resolute stride, Lia made her way to the main bedroom, her mind fixed on the impending confrontation. She paused in the living room, her eyes falling on her small, brown leather backpack. Without a moment's hesitation, she picked it up—a symbol of her unswerving readiness for what was to come.

With a sense of urgency, Lia ascended the steps, her hand diving into the bag for her cell phone. She retrieved the extra throwaway one that Frank had given her for emergencies, a clear sign of her complete preparedness for the impending confrontation.

She pushed one of the speed dial buttons while reaching for her duffle bag filled with her clothes. Shifting the backpack onto one shoulder and the duffle bag onto the other, she entered the bathroom and flipped the lock.

It wouldn't keep James out. She had discovered that little tidbit yesterday when she woke up before James and decided to shower without him. He had snuck in using his telekinesis on the lock and quickly joined her in the shower.

Lia shook her head, dislodging the erotic images streaming through her thoughts, and recentered herself. She realized the lock wouldn't keep him out, but at least she'd get a warning beforehand.

The call she dialed went through as she turned the shower valve on full force.

She figured the sound of the water would give her some shielding.

"Patterson," a deep voice answered.

"Josh," Lia babbled, the weight of the situation heavy in her voice. "James is determined to leave, but he's not ready. The stakes are too high."

"Understood," Josh replied with a heavy sigh.

"Frank gave me needles filled with a heavy sedative, but I don't feel right using them. Any ideas on how to reason with your bull-headed brother?" Lia leaned against the ledge of a large, porcelain ball-and-claw styled tub adjacent to the shower.

Quickly picking the first article of clothing her hand reached, she dragged on a pair of jeans.

"Yeah..." Josh replied. "But you won't like it any better than knocking him out."

"What?" Lia's voice trembled as she pulled James' shirt off. Her hand raised the still-warm fabric to her face, pressing her nose into the softness. Getting a good whiff of James' scent, she grappled with the thought of taking his freedom away. Her heart was torn between her mission to save him from himself and her love for who he was. The idea of drugging him felt like a betrayal, a violation of his trust, but she couldn't bear the thought of him leaving.

"Get him to chase you," Josh explained softly.

Sean crouched silently in the shrubbery close to the target's hidey-hole. He counted five men surrounding Suarez. Sean's group of six, stationed throughout this small neighborhood in Edgewood, MD, could easily overtake them, but he wanted to observe the meeting first.

It was obvious they were waiting for someone. Sean wanted to know who.

The communication in his earpiece sent him an update. "They look to be on the move," the voice in his ear spoke softly. "Should we intercept?"

"No," Sean whispered. "Stand down."

"Copy," the voice replied.

A few moments later, a dark gray Escalade pulled onto Nuttal Ave's side street into Harford Commons and headed their way. Sean had been counting on something like this to happen. The vehicle coaxed down the narrow road, turned into Lantz Street, and slowly eased up the driveway. The dark-tinted windows of the Escalade hid the interior occupants.

Sean raised his field binoculars to his eyes and viewed the hurried action from Suarez's men. The passenger door opened, and a slim figure stepped out. The form was female, but a large scarf around her head and dark sunglasses shielded her face from view.

But as the lady's delicate hand raised and grabbed her glasses, Sean got a look at the face.

To say he was shocked would be a mild understatement. The woman was someone he never expected to see in this situation.

"Team Alpha. Surround her and those men," he ordered as he got ready to move.

But no answering "copy" was given back. "Team Alpha, do you copy? Let's move."

Again, only silence remained in their communications, adding to the already tense situation.

Sean took out his device to check whether it was operating or not. Suddenly, a shadow silently eased across his position. When at arm's length away, the hard strike to his head sent stars flaring brightly in his eyes before everything faded to black.

"Say again?" Lia requested in a trembling voice, jerkingly stuffing James' shirt into her duffle bag. They were in a remote hideout, surrounded by water on three sides, and the only way out was the truck parked outside.

"Get in the truck and start making your way back home, or better yet, in the opposite direction." Josh paused briefly before adding, "Make sure to leave a note behind. James will forget all about us and start chasing you."

"Brilliantly done," Lia murmured.

"Remember to take this cell phone with you. Frank Marshall installed a GPS tracker," Josh instructed. "We will ensure you have a good enough buffer to keep him close but not catchable. Or at least until we can come up with enough reasons for him to stay with you instead of joining us."

"What about Sean? I heard the call between James and you earlier. Is he still radio silent?"

"Yeah… but that doesn't necessarily mean a bad thing. James is just being James, Lia. It's hard for him to put us at risk while he stays behind," Josh reassured, his voice a soothing consolation in the tense dilemma.

Lia sighed softly. "I understand. But he's not ready. He's just being bullheaded about it."

"Ah, duh. Don't you know him by now?" Josh chuckled. "Being stubborn is one of his good traits."

Lia stood up and brought her knapsack onto the makeup counter. She quickly moved items around to determine what she had and if she needed anything else.

Josh swore loudly. Looking down at the incoming message on his phone, he said, "Lia, gotta run. You know what to do. I'll call James and distract him for a few minutes. Get out now and be stealthy about it. Oh, and don't forget to bring a gun. Just in case."

"Got it," Lia confirmed. "I'm ready to go—call me when you talk sense into him."

"Give me a couple of minutes to deactivate the security panel. When you hear my call come through to James, it means it is all clear. Good luck," Josh said.

When he deactivated the call, he expelled with deep emotion under his breath, "We're all going to need it."

Chapter Eighteen

Lia left the shower running at full blast—a clever ruse to mask her movements. She carefully exited the bathroom, leaving no trace of her presence. When no one confronted her, she passed by the bed to leave the note and continued quietly downstairs, her escape plan unfolding with precision.

Lia kept a tight lid on her emotions and thoughts. Although she could tell it was James presently blocking her out from their telepathic link, she couldn't risk the chance of his barriers suddenly lowering.

With years of experience under her belt, her mental shielding ability would hold up just fine. What worried her more was accidentally throwing items with her telekinesis if she got startled rather than James penetrating her shields.

Lia shook her head, fearing it would be just her luck to give away her location by hurling a piece of furniture across the room.

She tried keeping a continuous loop of the five psychological functioning principles and their corresponding case studies running in her mind to stay focused. Highlighting the social and emotional dimensions, Lia began reciting the next phase of context when a growl emitted from the next room.

She instantly stilled, holding her breath.

When she heard James curse about the difficulties of securing a private airplane from D.C. to Virginia, her lungs slowly took in air. *Good,* she thought. Not only was she not discovered, but James' imminent departure appeared to be delayed. Relief washed over her, granting a moment of calm in the midst of her escape.

Spotting the keys to their truck on the console table in the dining room, her focus resumed. She crept in low on her hands and knees to stay out of James' line of sight. The kitchen cabinets would help keep her concealed.

When she was close enough, she took another steadying breath, slowly eased her hand up, and grabbed the key ring. Tucking it into her front pocket, she crawled backward toward the doorway. Using the doorframe, she carefully stood up and waited.

James' cell phone rang. Lia leaned forward, eager to hear the call.

"Josh..." James barked. "Do you have an update?"

Lia swiftly headed for the front door and carefully let herself outside. No alarms blared, no flashing lights went off. She eased the door shut silently. They had meticulously planned her escape, yet the unknown consequences of leaving weighed heavily on her. Regret pressed against the edges of her thoughts—was this truly the right move? Had Josh's careful orchestration accounted for everything?

Would her actions provide the distraction Josh anticipated, or would this cause more problems than solutions? As she jumped into the driver's seat, she prayed for the latter and held her breath one more time as the engine roared to life.

It was now or never.

The call from Josh delayed James for a little over ten minutes.

Unfortunately, without any new intel, Josh just repeated the same bad news from their earlier conversation. They still hadn't heard from Frank Marshall. Plus, recent communications coming in from Sean's earlier hacking efforts showed no new intel yet. However, this time, when disclosing that information, Josh's pace became much slower, hoping to give Lia time to put some distance between her and James.

Josh wasn't aware that this lack of further intel only cemented James' recent conclusion. James didn't need to be a part of the physical mission to lend a hand to his team. With

Frank's radio silence, they would need more coordination with the Intelligence office. The oldest Patterson sibling could be that link. Further consideration made James decide that going to Virginia with Lia to meet with the team was an even better plan.

Unfortunately, leaving that crucial part out of the discussion with his younger brother allowed things to play out accordingly. Too caught up in receiving any further intel, the placement of the parked truck and James' loud footfalls on the hard floor allowed Lia to escape without detection.

When the call was disconnected, James looked at his watch and noted the time. He wanted to talk to Lia before they left for the airport. He hoped to have a favorable update from one of his brothers by the time they were heading out.

Hopefully, he thought, *Sean's call will have better news.*

James took the steps two at a time. His breathing, although still rough, showed significant improvement.

"Lia, sweetheart," James called, pushing open the bathroom door. The water running resonated through the whole space like a small indoor waterfall, the sound bouncing off the tiled walls and floor.

As James stepped inside, the first thing he noticed was that there was no steam. With the lack of moisture in the air, it was easy to see the next important matter. Through the clear glass of the shower enclosure, he could see that it was empty.

Lia wasn't in there.

James quickly opened the shower door and reached inside to shut off the water. He turned back and headed into the bedroom. Moving nearer to the bed, he noticed a piece of paper on the comforter waiting for him. It was a note from Lia, but its contents were more than just a message.

James,

I'm going to the safe house where Frank is keeping my mom. I don't know where that is exactly, but I know once I'm on the road, someone—probably one of your brothers—will tell me the address. I don't want to wait here with whoever is assigned to babysit me while you put yourself back in harm's way. I pray you take care of yourself and return to me soon. I love you.

— Lia

"Shit," James cursed, his voice echoing in the empty house. As Josh had assumed, James' focus shifted to getting Lia back. He stormed back downstairs, his footsteps reverberating on the hardwood floor, and headed for the kitchen, his heart pounding in his chest. He hit redial on his phone, his fingers trembling with urgency.

"Josh, I have a problem."

"Yeah, I know. Lia just called me," Josh explained, playing out the plan he had constructed to keep his older brother away from harm.

"How far away is she?" James barked. "Do you have a trace on her? I've got to intercede and get her to the airport. I was planning on getting us both closer to you guys so I can head up the investigation. I can't be in the field, but I can be closer to the action... remotely if nothing else."

"Shit," Josh muttered urgently. "We thought you were heading out to get back in the field with us."

"What the fuck do you mean... we? Did you know she was leaving?"

"Uh, don't get mad... but I kinda told her to run away"

"What!" James roared. "Are you out of your fucking mind? She could be in danger!"

"I know! I know! You can punch me when you get here. She's got maybe ten minutes on you," Josh said. "By the time we get a ride to you, it'll be closer to thirty. But don't worry. I'll call her and tell her to pull over and wait. The good news is that I sent her in the opposite direction from your present location. There shouldn't be anyone looking for her around that area. She is safe."

"Where was that?" James interrupted as he shoved his gun into his shoulder harness.

"Smyrna, Delaware. It's about forty minutes away," Josh told him. "I'm sending you a bike. That will get you to her quickly and under the radar."

James swung around, snagged his backpack, and began stowing the ammunition rounds he had organized on the small table nearby. "I'll get the plane rerouted. There's an Air Force base in Dover. I need that ride ASAP," James ordered, his voice urgent and commanding.

"I had the Harley Cruiser en route as soon as I got Lia's call. You'll have it in ten minutes. The team, stationed outside of town, will bring it over to you. So don't yell at anyone."

"Copy," James replied and disconnected the call. He wouldn't make any promises; it was on them if they didn't get that bike here in the next five minutes.

But this present mess was on him. James combed his fingers through his hair and groaned. If anything happened to her, it would be all his fault. He forgot that he wasn't just making decisions for himself anymore. Lia needed to have a say in every decision from now on.

James should have explained himself much sooner.

Lia sighed; the burden of her anxiety pressing down on her felt like the weight of that backpack she had carried in the jungle.

Brian Patterson had just called and told her to stand down. Only eighteen minutes had passed, and she was halfway to her new destination. Lia released a loud groan in the truck's cab interior. Apparently, James wasn't rushing into danger as they had all thought—but she sure did.

Now, James was on his way to meet up, and together, they would catch a plane back to a small airstrip outside of West Virginia.

Spotting a good place to wait, she flipped on her signals and turned into the parking lot of Meding's Seafood up ahead. Slowing down, she exited Route One and stopped in the parking lot's back area. Looking around, she had a good view of the road.

The area was flat and plain, empty of heavy traffic and people. Other than this small retail building, no other businesses were nearby. The adjacent lot was filled with neatly plowed rows of dirt, ready for the next planting cycle.

Lia set the car in park. She lowered her head onto the steering wheel and let out a long exhale of tension. She hoped that by the time James got to her, he would have calmed down and understood why they did what they did.

As she raised her head to gaze into the rearview mirror, her phone began to ring. When spotting the caller ID flashing on the screen, she rushed forward.

Picking up the call, Lia's voice was strained with worry. "Frank, where have you been? Everyone is trying to get a hold of you." Her worry for Frank's safety was palpable in her voice, her anxiety reaching a peak.

"It's not Frank. It's your mother," Michelle Robinson's voice replied, trembling. "Frank gave me this cell phone and told me to call this number if he didn't return by now." Michelle sighed softly. "I've got this bad feeling something happened to him."

Lia gasped and fumbled with the phone, her heart pounding in her chest. She almost dropped it to the truck's floor. Once she set it down beside her, she grabbed the steering wheel and squeezed it tightly. "Okay, Mom. I'll let the team know."

"Where are you now, honey?" Lia's mom asked. "Maybe I should meet you there."

"I don't know, Mom. Let me talk to James and call you back. Are you alone? Do you have security with you?"

"Yes, dear. I think I'm fine. I'm just worried about Frank," she quickly replied.

Lia's protective instincts kicked in, and she felt a surge of concern for her godfather's safety. "Me too, Mom," Lia returned in a whisper. "Me too."

Chapter Nineteen

Pulling out of the fast-food drive-thru, Lia swiped the bag from James' lap as soon as he set it down. The aroma of fried food and cooking oil filled the truck's interior, and her stomach grumbled again.

She quickly rummaged through the bag as James drove around the parking lot, but he slowed and then stopped. Leaving the engine idling, James parked the truck and jumped out.

"Be right back," he said in passing, leaving the driver's door wide open.

Swiveling in her seat, Lia watched through the full glass rear window as James swung the tailgate down and climbed into the truck bed. He strode toward the fasteners securing the bike, giving the straps a sharp tug. After quickly adjusting two fasteners to a tighter tension, he jumped back down and slammed the tailgate shut.

When he slid back into his seat and shut the door, Lia handed him his food.

"All good?" she asked while munching on a fry.

"All good," James confirmed, stealing one of her fries from its container.

"Hey, get your own," she playfully complained, pulling back the bright red box with the large yellow M logo. She scooted farther away and repositioned the rest of her food on the dashboard—out of James' reach—a mischievous glint in her eyes.

She glanced at James before reaching for her wrapped junior burger.

"Lia, eat," James ordered. "Everything will be okay. The airport base is just down the road."

"I know," Lia said as she unfolded the paper from around her meal. She took a deep breath, inhaling slowly before letting it out. Relief washed over her now that they were back on solid ground. Obeying James' order, she took a bite of her burger, comforted by his care and concern.

James had seemed more worried about her safety than angry that she had left. When he had yanked open her car door— which, embarrassingly enough, she had left unlocked Lia's small frame —been instantly engulfed in his hard chest. He had held her firmly, rocking her from side to side, murmuring into her ear, "Promise me you will never do anything like this again."

She had been crying, unable to speak. Her heart had pounded in her ears, her breath coming in short, ragged gasps. But she had frantically nodded, pressing her forehead against his chest.

Now, with time to process everything, she realized they had both let their own fears and miscommunication create a misunderstanding. It had nearly driven a wedge between them. But after talking it out, they understood each other better than ever.

Once Lia's worry about James rushing into danger had eased—and she had a clearer grasp of what he intended to do about Frank—her stomach had made its presence known with a loud, resounding grumble.

The noise had made James laugh, easing her frayed nerves. She couldn't help but smile in response, and the two of them had immediately turned into the nearest fast-food restaurant with the golden arches.

James opened the container holding his grilled chicken sandwich, his eyes constantly scanning the windows. He had parked in a spot with quick exit access and clear sightlines, ever watchful.

Munching on a fry, he scrolled through an incoming message from Brian on his cell phone. "Brian says they contacted all of Frank Marshall's known informants. No one has heard from him in a couple of days. The last confirmed meeting was with a guy in Fredericksburg, Virginia."

"That's where I have my office," Lia commented, taking a big bite of her cheeseburger.

"Yeah, they made that connection too," James said. He leaned over, closing the distance between them, and licked a smudge of ketchup off her lips.

"Yum. Tastes good," he whispered.

Lia quickly grabbed a napkin from the bag and wiped her mouth. "Sorry," she mumbled, a pink hue creeping across her cheeks.

"Don't be. Like I said, you taste good." James smirked, then took a big bite of his sandwich.

As he chewed, he continued swiping through his phone, which he had placed on the seat between them. After taking a couple more bites and reading texts, he swallowed and said, "We'll be in Betterton by 1:00 p.m. Once we check in with your mom, I'll go through Frank's phone and send all the intel to Brian. We'll go from there. I don't like that two of our men are radio silent."

Lia gathered the uneaten portions of her burger and fries, placing them back into the bag. James intercepted the fries and dumped them into the lid of his sandwich container.

Smiling at him, she took a long sip of her soda. "Okay," she murmured around her straw.

A half-hour later, keeping a tight hold of Lia's hand, James boarded the helicopter. Dover Air Force Base housed one hundred and twenty military and support staff within its fenced perimeter and double that in the surrounding area. The physical contact with Lia helped keep James' mental shields strong around so many people. But that wasn't why he did it. His protective hold on her ensured her safety and kept the male interest to a minimum, providing a sense of security for them both.

Lia chuckled softly. "You have no idea how many female air-people were looking at your ass," she muttered while getting situated in the seat next to James.

James just shook his head in disbelief while reviewing the texts on his phone. "Brian says they have eyes on Herrera's men and are ready to follow."

"Good—maybe they'll lead them to Herrera, and we can get him too. The faster they're in custody, the quicker I can return to my practice."

James turned to Lia, his eyes filled with a mix of concern and affection. He swiftly adjusted her seatbelt, his touch gentle and reassuring. "We haven't really talked about what happens after this investigation. Your life's in Virginia, and I live in Annapolis but do a lot of traveling," James spoke quietly, his voice a soft murmur in the helicopter's hum.

His finger traced the soft, smooth area around her ring finger—of her left hand. His gaze moved up from her finger and zeroed in on her eyes. "You did mention two kids and a dog to me earlier."

Lia's blush, a delicate shade of pink, quickly spread from her face to her neck. She focused on the soft, comforting touches James was applying to her finger. "Well, I **did** have to get your attention. You were too preoccupied with bleeding all over the place," she muttered, her voice a playful tease.

"I love you, Lia," James said softly. "Will you move in with me when this mission is over? Or better yet, let me move in with you?" James' place was little more than an empty vessel where he dropped his gear off between missions. Nothing in it called it home for him.

Lia's gaze met James', her eyes sparkling with happiness. She nodded her head up and down. "Yes," she whispered, her voice filled with excitement, and a radiant grin spread across her lips.

"Good," James said in a calm, satisfied voice before turning back and looking out the small window. "Let's wrap this up, shall we?" he said while tapping his finger on the clear glass. He turned back and locked eyes with Lia before grinning back. "We have things to plan."

Lia looked down at her ring finger and smiled.

James reclined his chair back and reached to do the same to Lia's chair. He grabbed her hand after she was at the same level as him. With a slight squeeze in his grip, he said, "Get some rest; this trip is short, but try to get in a cat nap. We didn't get a lot of sleep yesterday."

Lia closed her eyes and grinned. She had to agree with him on that point. He was right. Sleep hadn't played a significant role in either of their time together. She felt that other, less pleasant activities would cause their lack of sleep in the following days.

Chapter Twenty

When Sean came to, the fast, jolting movement beneath him, combined with the throbbing pain in his head, made him want to chuck up whatever remained in his stomach. A groan must have escaped him because the engines went quiet, and rough hands yanked him up from the speedboat floor, forcing him onto a bench seat nearby.

Amado Herrera stood behind and slightly to the right of one of his men—the same man Sean had assigned to lead his small team back in Edgewood.

A malicious smirk twisted Herrera's features, making him look almost demonic. His once-handsome face was distorted by the flashing red and green lights on the bow of the boat. He gestured toward Sean, and the other man yanked him up onto the bench seat at the very back of the boat.

Sean tested the tightness of the zip ties securing his wrists.

What idiots. He thought, trying to connect with Josh telepathically. They had secured his hands in front instead of behind his back.

"One of the Patterson Brothers, huh?" Herrera jeered. "You're not so badass now, are ya?"

Without hesitation, Sean kicked his leg out, sending his traitorous ex-teammate overboard. The surprised grunt of the fallen man was the only sound before Herrera's scream pierced the night air.

The weight of his dire situation pressed down on Sean as he quickly sent a message to his brother. The tension in the air thickened, denser than a New England fog.

As Herrera shouted, "You die!" the gun went off.

In trouble, he sent to Josh telepathically as the cold burn of the bullet tore through his arm. The impact jolted him backward against the fiberglass coaming. Relief immediately overrode the pain—it had hit a non-life-threatening spot.

Report, Josh's voice came in sharp in Sean's mind.

Before Sean could respond or attempt to evade what was coming next, another gunshot rang out.

Sean knew this one was bad.

Pain exploded from his side. He staggered, the agony threatening to consume him. With a desperate burst of energy, he broke the zip ties around his wrists, the strain ripping a sharp cry from his lips.

Fighting through the pain, he moved toward Herrera, but the crime lord and another one of his goons got to the Patterson sibling first.

Sean struggled, but his strength was fading fast. His body tilted sideways, the sensation of falling dominating his senses.

The scent of salt and murky water filled his nose.

Just as he was about to hit the water, his head violently collided with the side of the boat. Lights flashed behind his eyes before a deep, consuming darkness swallowed him whole.

Sean didn't feel the water lovingly envelop him.

He didn't experience the coldness seeping into his skin, muscles, and bones.

He didn't hear the engines start back up or the boat as it sped across the bay, away from Pooles Island—because a warm pocket of air surrounded him.

The soothing, swooshing sound of water brushing up against an impenetrable barrier blended with the rhythmic beat of his heart. Everything remained silent except for the fading murmur of the distant motor—until even that was gone.

For a while, only an occasional fish jumping, the strong winds, and the lapping of waves broke the stillness.

Then something even more incredible happened.

The fast-moving, dark water—still protecting him—began to push Sean upward toward the boundary between water and sky.

Coughing, disoriented, and barely conscious, Sean was cradled by the water, as though wrapped in a warm blanket. The fast, shifting tide carried him along.

Time drifted away. One moment bled into the next.

Sean floated, unaware of how long he had been in the water. It felt like hours had passed, only for his mind to shift to thinking it had been mere minutes. The confusion looped endlessly, a cycle with no beginning or end.

Until something crept into his awareness, breaking the spell.

A rhythmic stroking reached Sean's ears, followed by a consistent beat hitting the water—soft at first, then growing louder and louder.

Suddenly, something small struck him. Sean groaned softly.

From the darkness, a shape took form.

A small boy in a baseball cap sat in a kayak.

"What in the world?" a voice exclaimed.

But it wasn't the voice of a boy. It was lyrical, breathy—not at all what Sean expected.

This voice belonged to a woman.

Sean tried to speak, but nothing passed through his numbing lips. Everything began to fade again.

In his last moments of consciousness, the water bubbled and churned around him, lifting him higher.

Capable hands grabbed at his body before the darkness claimed him once more.

"Hold on, whoever you are. I'll get you help," she had promised—a beacon of hope in the darkness.

Lia felt relieved when Michelle Robinson looked no worse for wear as she sat calmly in the chair opposite the sofa. Updating James on Frank Marshall's visit a day and a half ago, Lia's mother appeared impeccably dressed in pressed linen pants and a blush-pink silk shirt.

During the conversation, Michelle explained that Frank had been asking a lot of questions about John Robinson's work.

James knew this had something to do with Lia's ransom note.

Unfortunately, Michelle didn't have many answers to give— unless they were about the guest list for the many work-related dinner parties she had orchestrated over the years.

Michelle Robinson and Jenna Marshall had a lot in common in that regard. They handled their husbands' work associates and contacts like seasoned counterintelligence agents—because, in most cases, with their husbands' kind of work, they were.

Having facilitated many successful business dealings across a well-stocked and well-served cocktail party, both women knew how to work the room to their husbands' advantage.

"I told Frank that Aerial Dynamics Corporation got John's journals after the memorial service. I don't have any of his research at the house anymore. The last contact I got from Robert Evans was the company's Christmas card last year."

Michelle touched the edge of her collar, smoothing a crease before looking away.

"I don't like to think about John's work," she said softly.

That was more than understandable—Lia's father had died in a lab explosion.

With everything incinerated in the flames, Michelle hadn't even had a body to bury.

Clearing her throat, Michelle reached for the delicate, flower-painted ceramic teapot.

"Oh, dear, we need more. Let me go get us a refill," she murmured while easing off the sofa. She sent Lia a soft smile and added, "I'll be back in a jiffy."

Lia looked at James, who sat beside her on the sofa, his hand anchored to hers.

Four other guards were spread around the interior and exterior perimeter of the safe house. Happy to lend James her shields, Lia made sure he wasn't in any danger of an overload.

James grinned while managing to look refined, holding the delicate teacup in his hand.

"Got to make a good impression," he said before taking a quick sip of the lukewarm tea.

"James?" Michelle called from the other room. "Would you prefer coffee?"

"No, Mrs. Robinson, I'm good."

Michelle stepped back into the small sitting room as James shared a smile with her daughter.

He didn't see the small gun hidden behind the teapot in Michelle's other hand.

The shot rang out, and a dart hit James squarely in the chest.

James had no time to react. He slumped over, and the porcelain pink teacup slipped from his fingers, crashing onto the coffee table.

Lia gasped and reached for him, but one of Michelle's guards stepped in beside the older woman, raising a gun that looked similar to the one that had shot James.

He gestured with the weapon toward the sofa and shook his head.

"Sit down, dear," Michelle said softly. "We have lots to discuss."

Chapter Twenty-One

Frank Marshall viewed his present predicament with the dark humor his wife thought she had trained out of him years ago. Unfortunately, it was still very much a part of his nature, buried deep until moments like this—when she wasn't around to witness it—brought it to the surface.

He tugged on the steel chain that connected his ankle to the thick ring secured in the stonewall behind him. *That was new.* He would have noticed something like that when scouting this safe house.

Unlike most homes in this region, which lacked basements due to the sandy soil and high flooding risk, this one had a small cellar. Not that Frank's team would have needed to access it under normal circumstances.

Now, he was nothing more than a tethered old dog, unable to protect his family.

"Too bad, James. You're really missing all this," he muttered, his voice tinged with regret.

He tried to get closer to where James lay unconscious on the bed across the room, but the chain held him back.

Their captors had strapped an IV line to James' arm, administering a constant drip of some foul mixture. James hadn't moved since they had brought him down here.

That had been a couple of hours ago, Frank guessed. Give or take.

With a heavy sigh, Frank dragged his chain back toward his cot. He kicked the rusty bed frame repeatedly, the movement jostling the old mattress. The foul stench of mildew and sweat seeping into his nose.

"I owe Jenna a big bouquet of apology flowers," he said out loud, as if James could hear him. "She's been telling me for years that something was off about Michelle."

Frank glanced over to where James slept.

The male nurse—who doubled as their prison guard—had told Frank that Herrera had put James into a drug-induced coma before carrying him down here.

Knowing coma patients could sometimes hear voices, Frank had kept up a steady monologue between the guard's routine check-ins.

Glancing at his wrist before remembering they had taken his watch, he shook his head, slumped his shoulders, and sank onto his cot. The old springs let out a high-pitched, grating squeal, the sound clawing at his already raw nerves.

A chill settled deep in his bones.

"I'm an old fool, son," Frank murmured, his voice heavy with regret. "I never saw it coming."

The early afternoon sun shone brightly through the front sitting room's window. The light's angle coming inside cast abstract shadows on the floor. Lia studied the shapes while trying to connect telepathically with James.

Lia's gaze shifted to her hands, folded on her lap. Her mother, a master manipulator, flitted around the room, straightening one thing after another while further explaining her actions.

The revelation that her mother had orchestrated–with some help–Lia's abduction in Mexico was a staggering blow. All for the sole purpose of luring out Lia's father, a man who had been declared dead when Lia was a teenager.

But Lia's mother believed otherwise. These fiends had spread lies that John Robinson was alive. They also told her that Frank Marshall had been giving John updates on both mother and daughter over the years.

A barely-there groan escaped Lia's lips, a testament to the emotional turmoil she was in. No matter how often she tried to convince her mother of this falsehood, it made no difference.

John Robinson's wife wanted her heart's desire. She wanted her husband back.

Shaking her head at the absurdity of it all, Lia tried once more to connect with James, her heart racing. She refused to believe the blankness on his end. He was alive; she was sure of it. If she was alive, he must be too.

Michelle Robinson sat on the sofa by her daughter, her every move calculated. She patted Lia's hand a few times before sitting further back on the couch.

"So, dear, I knew your father would come for you if Frank was out of the way. We had the ransom note say to come alone and bring the power supply." Michelle tilted her head to the side and continued in a hushed manner. "Mateo Suarez wants the power module thingy. I just want our family back together."

Lia grabbed onto her mother's hand and squeezed softly. "Dad isn't here, Mom. He's gone. Those men are lying to you," Lia said in a whisper, her disbelief in her mother's actions evident. She felt a mix of frustration and pity for her mother, who was so desperate to believe in a reality that was no longer true.

Michelle just shook her head from side to side in quick succession before giving Lia a sad smile. "Frank Marshall was lying to us, Lia. He knew where your father was all along, and he kept us apart from him. I was given proof," Michelle remarked with a sharp glint in her eyes. "Frank is to blame. He took away John."

"Where's Frank, Mom?" Lia asked with a sense of dread.

Lia's mother just let out a puff of air and tilted her head back. She gazed up at the ceiling for a few moments before meeting Lia's gaze.

"Don't worry, Lia, Frank is fine. But I really don't care what happens to him later. He has gotten into bed with the wrong people... now he'll have to pay the price."

Lia tightly closed her eyes and shook her head, trying to wake up from this nightmare she was currently living in.

"Mom? What's happened to James?" Lia squeezed tightly onto her mother's hand. "Please don't do this, Mom," Lia begged as she raised her eyelids and met her mother's gaze.

"Don't worry, Lia. Your boyfriend will be just fine. As I told you before, I did what I could to ensure he stayed out of harm's way. I won't risk hurting you with the link you two share."

Michelle skimmed her fingers along Lia's cheek and smiled. She withdrew her other hand from Lia's hold and left.

"James is tucked out of the way and can't get himself killed trying to be a hero. Frank Marshall has told me many times over the years about James' heroic deeds."

Michelle smiled a dreamy smile and raised her finger to skim the pendant around her neck, a necklace that Lia's father had given her mother when Lia was born.

Lia's mother looked down and met her daughter's confused and worried expression. She wished for the right thing to say to relieve her daughter's concerns and assure her that things would work out splendidly. But the house had ears that couldn't get an inkling of her final plans.

Michelle was very determined to get her family back together.

A rapid knock on the front door had Michelle Robinson turning eagerly and heading out of the room.

"Lia, don't take to heart what comes next. Don't worry. I have everything under control." Her eyes held a manic gleam as she fluffed up her hair and checked her reflection in the mirror nearby.

Turning back toward her daughter, she raised both hands and gestured with both thumbs up. "Wish me luck," she commented before walking away.

Lia let her gaze follow her mother's exit until she was out of view. She quickly started to get up, but a deep throat clearing nearby had her hesitating.

She looked over her shoulder to the doorway between the sitting and dining rooms. The guard came further into the room and said softly, "Stay where you are."

Lia nodded once and looked away. Shortly afterward, she heard her mother's approach while chattering about "traffic and tardiness."

Stepping back into the room, Michelle smiled brightly at her daughter. "Lia, I want you to meet some old family friends."

Having had to sit in several briefings with James and his brothers, Lia recognized the two distinguishably dressed men standing just beyond her mother.

"Sweetheart, say hello to Amado Herrera and Mateo Suarez. They have some unfinished things to settle with your father. We are going to help them."

Michelle beamed with a broad smile and sparkling eyes. She showed no fear or concern about the men being here.

Lia sighed softly and let her gaze drop, resting on her tightly grasped, folded hands. She had no idea what mess her mother had gotten them into, but she prayed there was a way out.

"Miss Robinson, you are a vision of loveliness, just like your mother," Herrera spoke with a deep, resonating voice. His tone and presentation reflected the culture and gentle manner of his political position.

Still, Lia's mind became overwhelmed with an oily coldness that slithered across her shields like a snake moving in the grass to stalk its prey. This man's outward demeanor and appearance hid a dark evil.

Suarez stepped further into the room, reaching for Michelle's hand, which he kissed in an old-fashioned manner. Lia's mother giggled like a young schoolgirl.

From this older man, Lia felt the heat and cold mixed in equal parts within his mind. The calculation and righteous zealousness for a cause went hand in hand with this man. Lia also felt a want for more than just power from him. A sincere affection mixed in with all the rest, and Lia had a good guess who caused this emotion.

"Michelle, darling, it is a pleasure to see you again. We hope to have this matter cleared up in a day or two. Then we will let Lia get back to living her life. While you, darling, will get back to doing what you do best. Together, we will rise to the top within the Mexican government with the help of your ex-husband and Frank Marshall."

Michelle beamed with happiness and gave Lia a quick wink. "Just wait, Lia, things will soon be better than ever."

Lia looked toward her mother, horror flashing across her face as her panicked mind silently screamed.

Dear Lord—what is my mother up to...

Chapter Twenty-Two

Frank Marshall looked up from the old, faded magazine on his lap. The two single bare-bulb porcelain socket fixtures spread across the dank, unfinished area barely lit up the page. But it was more of a prop than actual reading material.

As the guard descended the steps, Frank discreetly slid the magazine onto the mattress. The guard's eyes never left him, his hand steady on the gun. The tension in the air was palpable.

Suarez had instructed the guard to be constantly ready when interacting with this prisoner. The guard's boss had greatly respected Frank Marshall and was about to get paid a handsome fortune for handing him over to an associate.

"Mr. Marshall, I've brought something for you to eat and drink," the guard said, raising the small cooler in his other hand. "Once I check on your friend, I'll slide it over to you. Please remain seated, and I won't have to hit you with another dart."

Frank just nodded once and kept his gaze on the man. He watched as the lackey quickly went to James' bed—his friend and partner in this dangerous game—and checked the IV line and the medical equipment beside the bed.

The guard placed his gun on the table beside the bed and raised his stethoscope from around his neck. Settling the device at his ears, he leaned over James' still form and listened to his heart rate while keeping a finger on the pulse point at the patient's neck. Easing the stethoscope down to rest against his chest, the lowest-ranking member of Suarez's team turned back and made notes on a clipboard by the bed.

Suddenly, Frank Marshall stood up and approached the edge of his cot. He kept his gaze locked on the guard, who now stood frozen in place.

"I want you to fix my friend's line so the degree of sedative is significantly decreased. Use your best guess on how low the dosage should be changed."

Marshall had beads of moisture coating his forehead and upper lip. This form of mind control took a lot out of him. But getting James awake was worth the risk.

The guard moved with stiff, robotic movements, as if his limbs were fighting against his mind's commands. His eyes, usually sharp and alert, now seemed glazed over, as if he was in a trance.

Frank strained against the end of his chain's length, every bit of strength his ability could handle centered on getting the guard to follow through on his order. By the time the IV line was altered and the drip monitor was changed to a new setting, Frank Marshall was trembling with extreme fatigue, his body slumping to the ground.

As Frank fell to the ground, the guard snapped out of his trance. His confusion was evident as he looked around the room, trying to make sense of what had just happened.

Turning to leave, he spotted the old man lying crumpled on the floor.

Picking up his gun carefully, suspecting a trap, he headed toward Marshall's form. When several light kicks to Marshall's shoulder got no reaction, the guard bent down and turned the prisoner onto his back.

Suarez's lackey quickly checked for a pulse and let out a relieved sigh upon finding one. The boss wouldn't be pleased if anything dire had happened to 'this' prisoner. Standing up and slowly backing away, he kept his gaze squarely on Marshall's unmoving frame the whole time. His gaze switched to James before turning back and studying Marshall again, his expression unreadable.

Then, with a shrug of his shoulders, the prison guard dismissed the fallen man and exited the basement.

Realizing his shift was almost over sprang to mind as he closed the cellar door. He sighed heavily, wanting a few hours of sleep.

Frank Marshall woke up with a quick jerk to his upper body. His hands slid slowly across the rough, uneven concrete surface and stopped close to his shoulders. His mind raced through recent memories, recalling what had happened earlier.

Pressing up, using the floor to push against, his upper body lifted off the damp concrete. A groan softly escaped as his joints and bones protested being exposed to the cold dampness of the floor.

Frank pushed through his discomfort and tried to stand. The movement of metal against a hard surface resonated in the room's silence. The chain and metal band around Frank's ankle gave him a dragging resistance with every movement.

There would be no guessing the time of day or how long he had been out, as there were no windows to the outside. For all Frank knew, the guard could have come and gone numerous times and just left him lying there alone.

Standing up too quickly, a dizziness immediately swamped his senses. Shaking off the sensation, he moved further away from the moored connection, and his chain grew taut.

His gaze focused on James' IV line. Frank soon realized he had no reference point from his location to gauge the young man's condition. James, his comrade in arms, lay there, a stark reminder of their dire predicament.

Frank's voice echoed in the room, a command that brooked no argument. "James, wake up!"

No movement came in response.

"James, get your ass up!" Frank demanded, a bit louder.

When he spotted James shifting slightly, Frank held his breath. After a slight pause, with no further movement coming from James, he barked again, "Patterson!"

James fought against the dragging pull of sleep and tried to get his eyelids to rise. But they refused to obey him. "Hm... umb be," he said softly, the words refusing to form properly on his lips.

"Fight it, boy!" Frank yelled out. "Wake the hell up!"

The oldest Patterson brother struggled to move. The light blanket covering him felt like a straightjacket, holding him in place. It took several attempts, and each time he tried, he managed to move slightly more than the last.

Trying again, he got his legs to shift higher this time. His one hand jerked up, but his other seemed to have less of a range of motion. He strained harder and felt stiff resistance, as though something was holding him back.

Suddenly, Frank heard the lock at the basement door move.

Frank quickly leaned hard against his chain, toward James, and spoke with urgency. "Someone's coming, son. Don't make a move or sound," Frank frantically ordered.

Praying James was lucid enough to follow orders, Frank made one more attempt. "Son, play dead. That's an order, soldier," he barked with all the authority he could muster in a harshly whispered voice, and he prayed it would work.

His message must have been conveyed because no further movement or sound came from James' vicinity. With a glance toward James, Frank hoped it stayed that way.

With great care for silence, Frank Marshall carefully returned to his cot and watched as the guard made his way downstairs.

Lia bounced in her seat with the acceleration of the boat's engine racing across the turbulent water. The Chesapeake Bay area was known for its quick tides and even faster-changing weather.

Their ship, a small trawler vessel, rocked and swayed with the choppy waves, the engine reverberating as sounds slammed against the water and the overcast sky.

When Lia and Frank were dragged onto this vessel, the sun had been bright, and as warm as a late October afternoon could get seasonally.

Now, the skies were cloudy with incoming rain. The temperature along the water had dropped by several degrees, and the wind made it seem colder. The chilling wetness seeped through the light jacket Lia's mother had given her. The storm was coming, and it was bringing with it a sense of urgency and danger.

Lia leaned back, easing away from the hardtop canopy to look overhead at the sky. The rain would probably start soon.

A quick pacing foot traffic made her gaze jump to Suarez, climbing the companionway steps from the quarters below. "Lia, would you prefer to wait below? You look cold."

Lia shook her head quickly back and forth. "I'm fine. If I go below, I'll get sick."

Suarez pressed his lips tightly together and nodded, understanding. Spending his early twenties as an officer candidate for Mexico's Navy fleet, he was used to being on the water. He never got seasick, but he could sympathize with Lia's plight. Suarez had seen many good, sturdy men fall sick after boarding a boat.

Lia had lied.

She didn't get seasick.

John Robinson had loved the water, and Lia was her father's daughter. Her dad had taken the family sailing every chance he could. She had learned to navigate these waters from her father, and later with Frank Marshall. This bond with the water was a part of her, a part she couldn't deny, even in this situation.

Although there was no reason for these guys to know anything about that bit of history. This knowledge gave her a slight advantage, and she needed to remain on the outboard deck to keep an eye on their surroundings. Knowing these waterways like she did would allow her to relay where they ended up and any other bit of information that would help the Patterson brothers.

She could sense James through their link. He seemed confused and went in and out of consciousness, but he fought the sedative's hold on him. By the time he surfaced—completely free—Lia hoped she would be ready to lend some assistance.

Suarez came to sit alongside her. He sympathetically patted her knee, but his attempt lacked sincerity. His emotions were filled with anticipation of grasping the prize. Plus, like her, his attention remained fixed on the surrounding area.

"How long until our destination?" he asked the captain, who was sitting at deck level at the navigation and steering helm.

"Shouldn't be much longer. I'd say within the next half hour," the captain replied, glancing at the navigation screen before resting briefly on Lia. His face held mild curiosity before switching his gaze to Suarez. He shrugged and added, "We should outrun the rain, but don't hold me to that."

Suarez just nodded back, his eyes still on the surrounding area.

Being off-season, the boat traffic mainly consisted of serious-minded fishermen, with the occasional National Guard vessel making its rounds and switching out scheduled shifts. One of their smaller bases was north of them at Still Pond Point. But Suarez was confident that as long as his men stayed at a moderate speed, they had no cause for concern.

Suarez looked over and met the captain's gaze. "Good. Once we dock at the small marina, you stay with the boat, and I'll have one of my men stay behind with you."

The captain nodded, pleased he was getting a nice chunk of change for chartering this vessel in the offseason. He hadn't asked too many questions and wasn't planning on remembering anything about this afternoon's trip if anyone came seeking answers.

Lia watched the two men interact. She knew she would get no help from the rough, rugged, and weathered seaman. His callousness and disregard for her and Frank Marshall were more than evident when they had come on board earlier.

Frank Marshall had been carried over the large guard's shoulder and quickly delivered to the lower quarters. The captain had just called out which cabin had a berth that could be used. His disregard for Frank's well-being or Lia's forced presence on the vessel seemed incidental to his bottom line.

Reaching over, Suarez patted her knee again in a fatherly manner. "Lia, I want you to stay behind with one of my men. There are several outbuildings close to the dock. We should be on our way once we trade with your father and Frank Marshall. If the weather gets bad, I'll arrange for us to return by car. I'll get you back to James, and you both will be free to go."

"Do you think I'll trust anything you say?" Lia's voice was sharp, filled with distrust.

"No," Suarez sighed. "But I do want to assure you. I mean you two no harm."

"But you can't say the same for Frank Marshall," Lia inserted softly, her words carrying a weight of uncertainty that hung in the air. "Do you honestly believe my father's alive? You may have got my mother fooled, but I'm not buying it."

Lia shook her head from side to side. "Whoever contacted you for this meeting, it wasn't him." She tried to have those words coated in confidence, but the doubt that edged into her mind bled thoroughly through, adding to the growing distrust between them.

Chapter Twenty-Three

Back at the quaint seaside cottage, Michelle Robinson leaned over, opening the oven door. The heat immediately rushed up and warmed the air around her.

Michelle, with her mind full of scheming thoughts, carefully transferred her freshly baked treats from the baking sheet to the raised metal grid at the end of the island. Her meticulousness was evident in every move she made.

The smell of rain was in the air, and the warm, freshly baked apple turnovers would be a nice accompaniment with coffee and hot tea.

Looking up as one of Herrera's men marched in, she smiled with her best hostess demeanor.

"I was slightly disappointed when Suarez and Herrera changed their minds about me going with Lia. But I guess this works too. This afternoon's snack will help warm everyone up with the temperature dropping." Michelle grinned, a brightness dancing in her eyes. "I'll have everything set out in a few. Why don't you hand me that large tray over there, and I'll load everything up? You can enjoy a cup of coffee in peace while I distribute these items to the rest of the men."

The large, middle-aged man with a rigid posture and a severely grim expression perpetually on his face held her gaze. But he nodded once before turning away to get the serving tray leaning against the backsplash further down the span of cabinets.

After doing as she asked, he stepped back closer to the center island and reviewed the choices before him. Reaching for the already cooled baked cherry tarts—done before this last batch—he picked one of the larger-sized cherry pastries and one apple turnover still warm from the oven. He set them both neatly on the prim napkin provided.

Michelle carefully set the tray down on the countertop.

"Let me pour you a cup of coffee, Mr. Beall," she commented, pulling off the flower-print oven mitts that matched her apron. "You take two spoonfuls of sugar, yes?"

As a perfect and reputed hostess, Michelle took pride in knowing everyone's preferences.

The man nodded, and Michelle beamed in her sunny, friendly manner.

"You have a sweet tooth, I see," she remarked, turning back to the large, industrial-sized carafes set off to the side by the long stretch of counter space to her right.

As the porcelain cup was filled, with the correct amount of cream and sugar added, she returned to the center island. She handed him the cup and said, "Go sit down and take a minute to yourself. I'll just fill the rest of the items on the tray and get out of your hair."

She smiled as she finished loading the paper plates, disposable cups, cream and sugar server sets, wooden stirrers, and two plates filled with baked treats onto the tray. Having already filled the portable serving carafes with coffee and hot tea, she also transferred them to the tray.

Mr. Beall sat down while looking around. Figuring no one would blame him for taking a small break, he took a big bite of his apple turnover and enjoyed a fine cup of coffee.

The guard watched in silence, admiring Michelle's graceful movements as she prepared to serve the refreshments. He found her elegance and poise relaxing to watch, a quiet joy radiating from her.

His sharp grunt seemed to please Michelle. Her smile increased two-fold, and while picking up the tray filled with her goodies, she practically glided out of the room.

The kitchen was quiet as the guard finished his coffee and pastry. He looked out the window at the rain, but the warmth and cheerfulness within the room remained. Michelle's calm demeanor seemed to permeate the space.

Suddenly, a crash of porcelain interrupted the quiet of the kitchen and the steady rain outside. The light tan liquid splattered on the dark gray marble floor, intermixed with shards of pink porcelain.

Mr. Beall slumped over in his chair, his head and upper body lying on the table's surface, his fingers still clutching the rest of his half-eaten pastry.

The basement lock eased open slowly, and Michelle carefully descended the rickety, wood-framed stairs. She held tightly onto the crude, wooden 2x4 that served as a railing. As she made her way down, her head shook from side to side, and a deep frown marred the ordinarily calm and steady features of her face.

Coming to the bottom step, she retrieved her cell phone and swiped the security pattern against the glass surface. The app she wanted was on the front slide and quick to activate. After viewing the information, her frown deepened, and she muttered something indiscernible under her breath. Turning slightly, she faced the large hospital bed holding James Patterson, then placed her phone back in her pocket.

Her hand stayed in the large pouch, shifting across the inside surface until it found the items she wanted. She quickly pulled out a needle she had stolen from Herrera's man—the one serving as the medic responsible for keeping James in the coma. The clear fluid inside should reverse whatever was currently being pushed into his system.

The young fool had been easily manipulated when she pandered to his enormous ego. Michelle's ability to exploit his weaknesses was both impressive and unsettling.

"James, I'm just so embarrassed with myself," she commented while walking toward the bed. She came to a stop at the head of the bed and carefully removed his IV line. She took the edge of the blanket covering his body and blotted at the bead of blood caused by the small puncture wound.

Waiting until no more blood seeped out, she tenderly brushed his hair away from his face.

"You could do with a haircut, James. It's important always to put your best foot forward."

Her face held a small smile, and her eyes studied James' features. She nodded a few times before a satisfying gleam reflected in her eyes. *Lia's man would be a good addition to their family,* Michelle thought, pleased with her daughter's choice.

She pressed the needle's point into his arm and pushed down on the plunger. When all the liquid had been emptied from the barrel, she removed the syringe and set it on the table beside the bed.

Sitting down on the edge of the mattress, Michelle Robinson studied James' relaxed face and waited—her patience a testament to the lengths she would go to see her plan through to completion.

A guttural, audible intake of breath came from James' mouth as he swiftly jerked up from a reposed position on the bed. His heart was pounding rapidly. He felt like he had just finished running a marathon.

Raising his hand, he tried to reach up to steady his spinning head. A loud clanging of metal rang out at the same moment he realized he was tethered to the bed rail by a pair of handcuffs. But his gaze didn't focus on what held him to the bed.

His eyes locked on Lia's mother, standing just within reach.

Michelle Robinson jumped back and held her hands up in a placating gesture.

"James, Lia is in trouble, and I need your help," she said quietly.

James swung his legs around and placed his bare feet on the floor. He quickly looked around the room.

Michelle stepped closer to the bed and gestured with her hand. Someone had placed his boots and socks on the table beside him. She lifted her hand, revealing the key to the lock around his wrist.

"Will you help me? Herrera will kill Suarez and Lia as soon as the exchange happens. He plans to make the trade with Frank Marshall and my husband using other associates instead," she explained, reaching for the restraint on his wrist. "They're almost at the boatyard."

James tried to use his telekinesis to release the cuffs, but whatever had been coursing through his system still blocked his control. He nodded once and raised his wrist.

Michelle carefully fit the key into the lock and twisted it. The mechanism opened with a click. She quickly stepped back, giving James room to rise. Her gaze followed him as he slipped off the restraint.

"Can you contact your brothers? The meeting is in two hours. We don't have much time to intercept," Michelle added, turning toward the stairs.

Lia? Where are you? Are you okay, baby? James asked through their telepathic link as he eased off the bed.

Oh my God, James! My mother—I'm so sorry. Lia hesitated before continuing. *Are you okay?*

Feeling Lia's panic rise, James' powerlessness surged.

James, tell your brothers we are heading to Gregg Neck's boatyard. It's on the Sassafras River, under the Augustine Herman Highway. Frank's in trouble. You have to get here!

Michelle turned back, sighed heavily while eyeing James' bare feet, then pointed to his boots.

"Get dressed. I'll explain on the way," Michelle ordered, turning to leave once again.

Chapter Twenty-Four

James swiftly tried to intercept Michelle's exit, but his balance was off. He collided with her, and they both nearly toppled to the ground.

Michelle quickly grabbed the wooden guardrail to keep them both upright.

James, are you there? What's going on? Lia's anxious voice vibrated within his head.

Needing to steady himself, James leaned heavily against the top railing.

I'm not sure what's going on. Let me find out, let my brothers know, and I'll update you. Please be careful; your mother said Herrera is up to something. He has someone there who will double-cross Suarez.

Ah... My mother is with you?

"You'll have to shake it off, James," Michelle reprimanded him. Her eyes glittered with urgent intent. "I need you to save my daughter." She pointed back toward the bed. "Now get your shoes on, and let's go!"

Lia's mother folded her arms across her chest, tapping a rapid rhythm on the hard floor with her foot. The sound perfectly emphasized her impatience with his lack of action.

"Mrs. Robinson, I'm contacting Lia now—"

"Is my baby girl okay?" Michelle clasped James' arm and squeezed it tightly.

"So far, she says she is—"

"We have to go. I need to be with my baby girl!" Michelle's voice trembled with desperation as she returned to the hospital bed. She snatched James' boots and carried them back to where he stood, frozen. Shoving the heavy boots into his chest, she turned and tried to head to the stairs, her movements frantic and determined.

James seized her arm and held on tightly, his voice gentle but firm. "You can't just rush up the stairs. Let me—"

"No need. I drugged their coffee and tea. I found some syringes in Lia's backpack. It should either knock them out for a long time or kill them," she said with a shrug.

A few seconds later, when James remained motionless, she narrowed her eyes. Fisting her hands, she rested them on her hips.

"Put your shoes on, James! Let's get out of here," she barked before hurrying up the stairs.

Stopping suddenly, she turned and flashed James a severe look, aggressively swinging and pointing her index finger at him.

"Hold on to the railing. I don't want you to trip, break your neck, and kill my daughter!"

Lia, your mother will not be invited to our wedding! James' ire was easily transmitted through their telepathic link.

While envisioning a future where Michelle Robinson was safely locked up in prison, James carefully made his way to the basement steps. Sitting on the wooden stair tread, he quickly pushed his feet into the boots and laced them up. With that done, he rose and headed upstairs, wondering what chaos awaited him upstairs.

The rain fell heavily, beating on the corrugated roof above Lia's head. Usually, she found the sound of rain soothing, but that wasn't the case right now. This relentless, bashing sound was deafening and only added to the pessimistic attitude she was fighting against.

For all intents and purposes, her mother was a traitor, and from knowing James' thoughts, there was a likely chance Michelle Robinson would spend the rest of her days in prison— or in a mental institution.

Not only had Lia's mother facilitated the capture of two special forces personnel, but she had also coordinated, through a black-market contact, the procurement and sale of a highly ranked officer to the Mexican government. Not to mention having her future son-in-law drugged and stashed in the basement of one of Frank's safe houses.

But James isn't incapacitated any longer, Lia reminded herself. With the situation now changed, the connection to James' siblings was just a thought away.

Keeping that good news in mind, she told herself to hold on a bit longer. If she knew James as well as she thought, he'd likely have an army of men storming this place within the next half hour—or hopefully sooner.

Lia tried to stop her teeth from clattering by biting down on her lips. She had no wish to draw attention to herself. She sat on an old metal chair with one leg shorter than the rest, causing a rocking motion when she leaned her weight from side to side.

The building they were kept in was just a few rows from where the boat was tied off, close to the diesel fueling station. The old, dilapidated structure housed various facilities for everyday operation. Lia glanced at the supply shelves filled with tackle boxes, miscellaneous tools, and packages of buoys in all sizes and colors. Aside from the ropes and buoys, most items were unrecognizable to her.

Shifting as far as she could while still remaining seated, she familiarized herself with her surroundings. Each visual tally would help the Patterson brothers when they arrived.

They had positioned Lia's chair in front of the office's double doors, which also served as a snack shack for the marina. A sign in the window confirmed this, with the store's hours listed on faded cardboard. Several changes had been made using scraps of paper taped over the original times.

Another sign reading **Closed** swung in the window of one of the doors. It still rocked from when they had dragged Frank's body into the area beyond and secured the doors with a padlock and steel cable.

Suarez and three other men had headed out, leaving her alone with a single guard—a guard who now showed blatant interest in her.

She was soaked to the bone from their trek from the dock. Water still dripped from her hair, further saturating her clothes. The jacket her mother had given her was useless. It was just a windbreaker, not a raincoat, and had done more harm than good.

The heavy rain had drenched the guard's clothing as well, and the stench of his body odor overwhelmed her despite the distance between them.

Lia removed the coat and wrung out the soaked fibers, hoping to generate some body heat by putting it back on. Her thin, long-sleeved, pale green T-shirt clung to her breasts and stomach. Her simple cotton bra was soaked through, leaving nothing to the imagination.

The guard didn't hide his interest in what he saw. He licked his lips and followed the shape of her upper body with his eyes.

She felt his menacing intentions creep into her mind. This man wanted to do things to her body that sent cold chills racing across her skin—chills that had nothing to do with the weather.

Quickly squeezing the excess water from the oversized jacket, she put it back on. It served more as a deterrent to the guard's gaze than any kind of warmth, but she still wrapped her arms tightly around her upper body and sat back down.

She grimaced when the man's smile revealed cigarette-stained teeth. His overlong hair, plastered to his skull and neck, made him look like a Halloween skeleton. The realization that something would need to be done if he moved closer settled like a weight on her chest, constricting her lungs.

Lia had to hold on until James and his brothers could get to her. With every fiber of her being, she believed they would arrive in time.

The tilt of her chin and the way she tightened her arms across her chest showed she was preparing for a confrontation.

Watching as the guard licked his lips and jeered at her for the hundredth time, she reminded herself of one crucial thing.

I am not helpless.

As he pushed away from the wall and sauntered toward her, Lia got ready to do what needed to be done. She took a slow, deep breath and drew the swirling energy in her mind into crisp focus.

I hope this works.

That silent prayer urged her on.

Chapter Twenty-Five

Josh Patterson swung open the helicopter door and jumped out of the interior cabin with two other men. His eyes, filled with a mix of relief and steely fierceness, glinted as he swiftly grabbed onto his older brother, James. The two, bound by a strong and unbreakable bond, shared a powerful embrace that lifted James' body several inches off the ground.

"Watch the damn blades, you idiot," James shouted, his voice a mix of relief and brotherly affection, as he slapped Josh's back.

The chopper's blades slowed to a lazy spin with the engine shut down—a sign that one small part of this dangerous plot was over.

James had also secured another small victory in this tumultuous situation. When he awoke, his new empathic ability had no adverse effect, thanks to Michelle drugging all the men inside the cottage. A fact that brought a wave of relief to James' younger brothers.

Unfortunately, that small advantage didn't last long.

The pounding pain gripping James' mind now told another story since his rescue. His faltering control to keep his mental shields in place tore at his endurance. He nodded to the two men standing off to the side of the cabin's opening.

The swoosh of a car door sliding open drew James' attention. An agent, who had ridden with them from the safe house, pulled Michelle Robinson from the back seat of a dark gray SUV.

Brian Patterson had swiftly arranged for a small special forces unit—a team of highly trained and dedicated individuals—to meet at Michelle Robinson's safe house location. Once there, they took Michelle into custody and raced to this adjacent field, far from the marina, to rendezvous with Josh. The trusted counterparts had enough sense to keep any witnessed incidents involving the Patterson brothers' specialized abilities to themselves.

Another team of two would continue with Herrera in custody, delivering him to the D.C. detainment facility before linking back up with the rest of the team at the marina.

Well... *all except Sean.*

James quickly shut down that train of thought.

He squared his shoulders with unwavering determination. With his jaw clenched and a flash of unyielding resolve in his eyes, James squeezed Josh's upper arms—a silent promise of their shared strength.

Josh nodded before pulling back. He gestured with his hand toward the waiting transport.

James jumped onboard and stood within the threshold of the cabin.

The helicopter could seat nine passengers in the main compartment. Three bucket seats sat side by side, facing away from the cockpit toward the main cabin. Three more mirrored that row, forward-facing, with a final row of identical seats behind them.

Michelle Robinson was brought alongside and held just outside the interior. With help from the guard, she was carefully lifted and placed in the large cabin.

Josh stepped off to the side and tapped the earpiece in his ear. Giving a quick update, he spoke softly while James got Michelle settled.

They maneuvered Michelle into a seat in the second row by the far window, and James fastened the harness around her upper chest and waist. The zip ties on her wrists, still behind her back, remained in place. No one was taking any chances of underestimating what Michelle might do again.

James had seen firsthand the level of determination this woman would exert to get her way.

When the small unit showed up at the safe house, they had been able to apprehend Herrera and his men. They had all been alive.

But judging by the blank look on Michelle's face, it wouldn't have mattered if they had all died.

Especially Herrera, who had screamed and raged after being revived by James from his drug-induced nap. Michelle had just kicked him hard in the stomach before letting the soldier escort her from the house.

James locked the fastener in place and returned to the threshold.

"Tim," he said, lowering his hand and reaching outward. The field agent from the special forces team on guard duty clasped James' hand and got a swift boost up.

"Sir," the man said with a jaunty grin and a slap on James' arm. He quickly took a seat directly opposite Michelle, behind the co-pilot's seat.

James jumped down and stood beside Josh.

"Report," James ordered.

"Brian and the team are en route, just outside the facility. They'll cover the entry points on the northeast side. We'll make our way through this field and the surrounding neighborhood. The marina is at the end of the development. Most homes are seasonal, with a few full-time residents. There's a SEAL team already deployed in the water along with a boat at the dock. They'll make sure no one escapes through that route."

Nodding, James' gaze turned back to Michelle.

She turned slightly in her seat, pulling her gaze away from the young guard to clash with James' intense study.

James now understood that Michelle's warm and friendly smile was just a façade. The realization of why he hadn't struggled to keep her emotions in check earlier dawned on him: Michelle Robinson was what clinical professionals termed a high-functioning sociopath. This revelation sent a shiver down his spine, and he couldn't help but break eye contact with Lia's mom.

Knowing Lia's assistance was helping his mental shields stay in place made every one of James' thoughts open to his life partner. He felt Lia's regret and sadness.

Don't. Sweetheart. James pushed through their link, sending a warmth of acceptance and love back to her. Taking a deep inhale, he tried to center on the mission rather than Michelle Robinson's consequences, which would profoundly affect Lia.

The oldest Patterson brother turned and met Josh's intense study. Bound to James through their sibling telepathic link—a profound bond that allowed them to share thoughts and emotions—Josh was acutely aware of the personal stakes involved in this mission's outcome.

"Lia and Frank are being held in the outbuilding, furthest from the large workshop building," James instructed, putting aside his troubling conclusion regarding Lia's mother. "You take point. My priority is to get Lia and then find a place to lay low. Mrs. Robinson said the meeting would take place in one of the mechanic's workshops. Ensure the rest of the men meet up with Brian and look for Suarez and his men. You'll want all eyes on the target. You secure Frank, meet with Brian, and lead the teams."

Josh nodded slowly while his gaze studied his older brother. Looking for regret or uncertainty in his brother's features or mind, Josh was amazed when he found none.

The second-oldest Patterson brother turned his gaze toward the edge of the field. But his attention wasn't on what was shown beyond the turned soil. His mind struggled to comprehend the sudden 180-degree turn James had taken regarding any mission—a shift that was as unexpected as it was disconcerting.

This mission, Josh acknowledged, realizing the full weight of the task at hand, especially now that his brother and Lia's lives were linked together. If either part of that couple should come to harm, it would affect the other. If death claimed one, the linked partner would fall as well.

We won't let that happen. Josh's resolve became fixed on that outcome. Switching channels to connect to the teams en route— as point-man—Josh relayed the new orders to the teams.

James switched his attention from Josh's daunting expression back onto Michelle Robinson. It was still unbelievable that this "Betty Crocker from Hell"—a nickname fitting for one's obsessive focus on perfecting hospitality in all things—was coordinating this whole operation, from Lia's initial kidnapping to what was taking place on Kent Island. It had equal importance to preparing the best culinary spread.

Except for what happened to my brother, Sean, James thought, knowing his youngest brother's absence weighed heavily on them all.

Michelle had ecstatically denied knowing anything about Sean's disappearance. She said that after overhearing what Herrera had arranged regarding his double-cross with Suarez, she didn't doubt that Herrera was responsible for Sean's disappearance, too.

Only death could sever the brothers' telepathic link, and their connection to Sean felt different—like an empty void. Josh had likened it to when James was drugged into a coma.

So, they all took hope in that—for their brother's survival— clinging to the belief that they would find him and bring him back, no matter the cost.

James and his brothers were resolute in their mission to capture Herrera's men alive. But after they got their answers—to help get Sean back—James didn't care what happened to them afterward. Their determination was steadfast, their focus clear.

The Patterson brothers had a job to do.

Chapter Twenty-Six

Lia sat in quiet determination, conserving her energy. The task of helping James erect his barrier from the onslaught of other people's emotions added another layer to her already complicated predicament, but she remained purposeful.

She braced for action when Suarez's man came for her—for the second time.

Knowing her telekinesis power was so unpredictable, she had gone with her empathic ability instead. This time, she used it in a more aggressive manner than she had ever done before. As a dedicated therapist, she did hold a tiny grain of regret for afflicting harm like this, but it became insurmountable compared to the need to protect herself. Her empathic powers were her lifeline in this dangerous situation.

The young man's quick and sure stride slowed to a stop once more. But this time, he backed up, stumbling and hitting the wall by the front entrance. With her empathic suggestion streaming into the guard's mind, Lia kept him loose and pliable.

Lia's gaze shone bright with glittering power. With her shoulders back and her hands fisted, she kept her sights on the target. Energy surged through her mind, and she focused it on her persistent, would-be assailant.

Sensing Lia's need, James sent his strength through their link. *You got this, baby*, came through loud and clear, telepathically. His confidence infused her with more determination to get this right.

James slowly eased his head down. The earlier rain had stopped, but he still felt the water easing down his jacket's collar and soaking his shirt. He felt the cold prickles of static electricity coat his mind.

On the brink of rescuing Lia, James found impatience disrupting his focus. He exhaled slowly, trying to regain his composure. It was a cruel irony that these external emotions—something he had always considered a weakness—now had the power to overwhelm him. The sheer difficulty of dealing with these emotions was a revelation he never expected, and it made his struggle all the more real and relatable.

Hadn't James and his brothers succeeded in the most expedient manner, regardless of the chaos surrounding them?

Hadn't James exceeded everyone's expectations, using logic and cold facts?

Hadn't James' modus operandum for keeping wayward emotions locked down served him well? Primarily for those rescued on all the missions Frank Marshall sent him on.

Clear thinking made all those assignments successful.

But now, when James needed his legendary control the most, it seemed out of reach. His normal compartmentalizing of those externally erratic emotions around him failed to work.

The problem wasn't just the onslaught of everyone else's emotions, although they were certainly taking their toll. It was Lia—and the way she made James feel—that was the real challenge. She was more than just another mission, and that realization made James shake in panic.

Of all those times in the past, as James, alongside his brothers, had been a beacon of hope in countless life-threatening situations, his duty to help others stood unwavering. But there were other desires stirring within him. Now, he understood the wisdom in the advice his parents and Frank Marshall had given him about finding a balance—a lesson that had always seemed distant but now felt painfully close.

I want that with Lia. The two kids and a dog sound really good to me, James admitted to himself.

And with that want came the realization of having something to lose. This changed everything.

A sharp, seizing pain shot to his head. Trying to shake it away, James grimaced and moved his head quickly from side to side. His will and love for Lia spurred him to find more control.

The various emotions continued to press into his mind from so many sides. But the fear that Lia tried to hide hit him the hardest. He gritted his teeth and struggled to keep his shield in place while giving Lia more power.

He had given little thought to sacrificing himself for the mission's good in his past, but he couldn't do that now. Lia would be sacrificed too.

This world needed more people like Lia, James thought.

This empathic ability made James feel so many tangible emotions. It became difficult to filter them from his own—made him realize just how much he had held back from everyone before Lia came into his world.

We are in position. Brian's message came through the brothers' connection.

James could feel his brother's worry—Josh's too. But James couldn't send any communications back to alleviate their concerns, becoming so focused on sharing all his strength with Lia.

Copy. James and I are just outside the dock's office and general store from where Lia reported on Frank Marshall's location. Moving to intercept, Josh sent through their link.

Copy, Brian replied back. *No one has come close to the main building. Just Suarez and one of his men are waiting inside. Two are standing guard at the front. One is at the back entrance of the 'boatyard's servicing shed.*

What about the docks? James managed to send through their link, but another sharp spasm went off like fireworks in his head. His nose started bleeding again.

The SEALs team is in place. This place looks deserted of civilians, Brian replied back.

"Shit," James cursed, pinching the end of his nose. That short telepathic message to his brothers had caused internal damage to his brain. He pressed the blood into the palm of his hand and then flicked the excess off.

Josh quickly intervened. *James, stop trying to send out communications. Just keep the line open; I'll do the heavy lifting, old man.* His use of humor helped ease some of the seriousness.

James just shook his head from side to side. He could practically feel Josh's smirk in his mind. However, a warm wave of energy flowed from Josh to James' mind, shoring up the cracks in his shields.

Okay, making my way around the back entrance. You got the front. Meet you in the middle. Let me know the minute someone shows up at the house. Out.

Copy. Out, Brian broke off contact.

The area around them gathered in thick clouds, and visibility extended to just a yard or two in front of them. James was thankful for small favors. If this fog had rolled in ten minutes ago, they would have had a problem landing the chopper.

Across that short distance, Lia watched as the vile man's gaze became unfocused. His body slumped back. Leaning against the entrance's doorway, he raised his hand and slowly wiped his face. The lack of energy to care about anything pulsed through him.

Finding this pocket of repressed memories to manipulate came as a shock. She hadn't thought this henchman held the ability to feel sorrow or loss. But fortunately for Lia, he did—and she squeezed every little bit of it to her advantage.

She sent the guard's thoughts back to the day of his grandfather's funeral. The sadness of loss from the only person who ever cared about him continued to bombard his mind.

Squeezing his eyelids tightly closed, James took a few deep breaths and let the air out slowly from his tight lungs. Lia's meditation technique had quickly become an important tool, helping him push most of the other people's emotions away from his mind. But the manipulation force Lia was extending to Suarez's man—and, in turn, the emotion the young man projected outward—was kicking James in the butt.

James' gun hand shook. He lowered it and tucked it into the waistband at the small of his back. He could do more harm than good with the weapon at the moment.

Where James needed to go came with complications. The raised plywood substrate, one-story building was built half on dry land and the other half on dock pylons—wood and steel frames, and wood-planked decking over water. The planked dock had some areas of new wood but primarily consisted of old, faded lumber that was far past needing replacement. Placing one's step on the unstable structure could cause a person to snap a plank in half.

Concentrating on putting one foot in front of the other with minimal sound and without falling through took everything he had. He needed to get to the threat before both of them ran out of juice. He carefully approached the propane tanks, sensing Josh coming from the opposite side.

He eased his way around the prominent display of fishing lures and netting just as the man slid down the wall. Seeing his chance, James shot forward with a spurt of speed.

The guard's body slid down the siding until his butt plopped onto the wide-plank unfinished wood floor. He tucked his legs in, wrapping his arms around them and hugging them close to his chest.

Lia continued to layer the sorrow in his mind to multiple extremes, until Suarez's hired thug's head became too heavy to remain upright. Lowering it, resting his forehead upon his folded arms wrapped around the top of his knees, he couldn't stop his shoulders from shaking with silent sobs. His tears mixed with the rain's wetness, falling in rivers down his face.

When the guard rolled his head to the right, his gaze came face-to-face with a giant, fierce-faced warrior marked with streaks of camouflage on his skin.

James' frame angled downward, and his nose was inches from the despondent guard. For a split second, his gaze mirrored the guard's bleak sorrow—before morphing into a cold, blank façade. The only telltale sign of discomfort was James' clenched jaw and the drops of blood falling from his nose.

Then the guard's eyes saw no more. A quick hit on the head sent everything into darkness.

"You should have remained on the helicopter," Josh whispered harshly to his brother. He returned the gun he'd used to knock the guard out to the harness at his side.

James wiped the smear of blood off his face.

Lia rushed toward him. Her immediate touch brought strength to his mental shields, and James felt an instant wave of relief.

Her breathing was harsh and strained, beads of sweat covering her face and body. Even as the temperature dropped with the coming night, James could feel the trembling in her muscles.

Nearly exhausted himself, James knew they had to move.

Squeezing her hand briefly, he pulled away from her grasp. "Lia, I need both hands to fight. But your closeness helps, honey. It'll have to do."

"James, there's hemorrhaging. You can't keep this up!" Her voice was saturated with panic.

"Let's get Frank and you out of here, and then we'll let my brothers take over," James promised.

Lia nodded quickly. When Josh tapped her left shoulder, she moved in the direction of his light touch, stepping aside. After maneuvering around her, Josh ascended the two steps, approaching the threshold that imprisoned Frank Marshall.

Grabbing a pouch from his back pocket, he knelt and began pulling out lockpicks, focusing on the padlock securing the doors.

"Step back," James ordered, fearing time was too crucial to waste. Raising his hand, he released a wave of telekinetic energy. The door exploded inward. But James' waning strength affected the finesse of his power—debris scattered everywhere.

Josh turned to his brother and saw fresh pain reflected in his eyes. "Bro, it would've taken me two seconds to unlock it. Don't push yourself unnecessarily. We're a team."

"James, please," Lia coaxed gently.

Nodding, James leaned against her. He raised his right hand and waved it toward the door. "Get him," James ordered. His breathing had grown heavy. Puffs of crystal mist formed around his mouth and rose into the air. Moving away, he pulled Lia out of the 'doorway, anticipating Josh's next move.

The thick, heavy mist lingered around them. Its damp weight settled on their skin, chilling them. A slight wind stirred the surroundings—ropes creaked on nearby ships, and maritime tools hung from hooks swung gently. Those sounds added to the eerie atmosphere. With visibility limited to a flickering ceiling bulb—its connection faulty—the area felt cloaked in ominous tension. Both Patterson brothers knew how exposed they were if the fog shifted.

Josh moved with painstaking caution through the debris. He disappeared into the store's interior darkness. But moments later, his tall frame reemerged at the threshold, a heavy burden slung over his shoulder.

In the dim glow of the outbuilding's portico, all could see Frank Marshall's hands and ankles were bound in harsh metal cuffs—a stark reminder of the danger that lingered. Suarez, a notorious criminal mastermind, was nothing if not ruthless. The extraction team was intent on keeping their advantage before their presence was discovered.

Josh adjusted Frank's weight in a fireman's hold, then drew his sidearm from its holster.

James pulled another gun from the concealed harness on his leg and handed it to Lia.

"Take off the safety and be careful with that," he said, grinning slightly as he gestured to the weapon. He reached behind his back and drew his own gun.

Lia nodded. She flicked off the safety and pulled the slide back with her palm. Turning her body sideways to the weapon, she kept it pointed safely away from the others. Frank Marshall had instilled gun-handling skills in her from a young age, and she knew exactly what was required in this high-stakes situation.

Chapter Twenty-Seven

The same eerie fog—thick and heavy off the water—coated the ground surrounding the two outbuildings. Clear sightlines extended only a few feet ahead. The rest was filled with a light-gray wall of clouds, creeping slowly along the ground as if it had a life of its own.

It reminded Lia of a Stephen King novel, the way the mist drifted apart—becoming briefly transparent—before thickening again to blanket the space around them. The outbuildings, just yards away, faded in and out of view, ghost-like from one moment to the next.

James and Josh, their vision obscured by the unnatural fog, were forced to rely more heavily on their other senses and combat training. Every step became a test of their field-honed instincts and heightened awareness.

Where Lia heard only the chaotic soundscape—the unrhythmic squeaking of the dock platform as water slapped against shifting piers, the groan of old wood and rusted metal rubbing together—James and Josh perceived more.

They picked up faint water movements washing ashore, the subtle swells rocking the boats, the scraping of multiple hulls against cushioned fenders. High-pitched whistling came from metal fasteners striking rigging, strung along booms and mainsheets of the nearby sailing vessels. Sharp snaps of flapping flags cracked through the mist, a staccato rhythm among the atmospheric symphony.

Fully aware of the danger, James dared to lower his mental shields further. He expanded his empathic scan outward, absorbing the psychic impressions of the fog-shrouded space. This newer ability—an evolution of his empathic gift—allowed him to differentiate friend from foe in the obscured chaos. But it came at a steep cost. The more he opened himself to the psychic currents, the greater the toll on both him and subsequently, for Lia. The potential consequences of this risk were enough to make anyone anxious.

Lia instinctively linked with James, anchoring his mental presence to her own. Her years of exposure and naturally developed and fortified shields protected her from the worst physical blowback. But she exercised severe caution—there hadn't been enough time for James to rebuild the proper protections that might buffer him from absorbing harmful psychic energy through prolonged contact with multiple targets.

James sent a silent message to Josh, now that Lia's presence gave him some added protection:

Our enemy is toward the east and west sides—gathering around the neighboring outbuilding entrances. You've got a clear path slightly to your right to get to Brian. Lia and I will pull back and keep eyes on the main office.

It was here that the brothers parted ways.

Be careful, Josh ordered, before disappearing into the fog in the direction James had indicated.

Lia leaned heavily on James. The energy she extended to him was quickly depleting her own reserves.

Stop it, James ordered through their link. *Don't push yourself.*

Lia's chin angled upward, her teeth clenched. *We are in this together,* she reminded him. *I won't let you carry this burden alone.*

James clenched his jaw and kept the groan to himself. *Woman, you are so stubborn!*

Ditto, Lia replied.

She shifted her weight from one foot to the other, leaning against the siding of the aging structure. Her gaze scanned the surrounding area, though the heavy mist obscured almost everything. Turning her head, she could barely make out James' grayish silhouette beside her.

Where is my mother? Lia asked.

She's back by the helicopter, in a neighboring field. We needed to make sure they didn't hear us coming.

Lia nodded instinctively before realizing the gesture couldn't be seen. *Okay,* she replied through their link.

A few quiet moments passed. In the distance, they could hear only the faint murmuring of men talking by the main office, but Lia couldn't make out what they were saying.

James pulled her closer and held her tightly, whispering in her ear, "It will be over soon."

"Boy, stop hovering over me," Frank Marshall grumbled in a faint whisper.

"Just checking your pulse, sir," Josh answered softly.

Frank waved his hand away and started to sit up.

Josh tried to ease a hand behind Frank's head to assist, but a low growl nearby had him quickly leaning back on his knees. With his hands resting on his hips, he carefully watched his commanding officer, ready to intervene if needed.

Frank Marshall slowly sat up—a sign of his recovery—and took in the surrounding area.

Josh had brought Frank to a secluded spot Brian had scouted just off the marina's edge. The area resembled a graveyard of sorts, with old boat parts stacked against dilapidated hulls of inoperable vessels, scattered and seemingly forgotten. The air was heavy with the smell of salt and decay, adding to the foreboding atmosphere.

However, Frank could make out nothing beyond the soupy mist. He shook his head, trying to clear the lingering fog coating his mind, then met Josh Patterson's gaze just inches away. The concern in Josh's eyes was unmistakable, adding to the tension in the air.

Frank didn't like seeing that reflected in the younger man's face.

Catching Frank's exasperated growl, Josh quickly schooled his features to a neutral expression. He silently rocked back on the soles of his feet and sprang up from where he had administered the small dose of adrenaline just moments before.

Two medium-sized spheres of wetness soaked his pant legs.

Frank's open palms rested on the small medic tarp Brian had spread out before they'd lowered their then unconscious superior officer onto it—something Frank quickly surmised had saved his back from a similar soaking.

"Report," Marshall growled. He didn't like how rusty his voice sounded.

Josh leaned down and extended his right hand toward his commander-in-chief while informing him, "Suarez is in the mechanic workshop with two men. We're waiting for their contact to show. We've got several teams throughout the area. One team of five surrounds the branched-out docking walkways. They have eyes on the front and east sides of the maintenance building. The other two teams of three are around the smaller outbuildings, watching the back and west sides. They've already subdued Suarez's men around the perimeter."

"A chopper is waiting, and a team of two is standing ready with Michelle Robinson," Brian added, swiftly folding the medical tarp and stuffing it back into his field sack.

"What of my goddaughter?" Marshall sighed heavily, then took the outstretched hand. After carefully standing and testing his steadiness, he turned and met Brian's gaze—who had returned to his previous task of scanning the surrounding perimeter, gun poised and ready.

She's with James," Josh continued, "near the—"

A low mechanical humming interrupted Josh. A flashing green glow of bright light made the fog appear like pea soup, whirlpooling above their heads.

Frank stepped clear of an old sailboat's hull, looking up into the sky and around the area, but the poor visibility revealed no clues.

The phenomenon lasted for a couple of minutes, then faded, leaving behind a stillness that weighed heavier than before.

A swirling movement out of the gray mist revealed a man standing just yards away.

Both Josh and Brian raised their weapons at the new arrival.

Frank Marshall swiftly stepped near them with a harsh but quiet order. "Stand down." He tugged first on Josh's arm, guiding the weapon toward the ground, then did the same to Brian's.

With that done, Frank faced the stranger, who began walking carefully toward them.

Chapter Twenty-Eight

The mechanical humming in the sky, with the soft green glow of lights, disappeared as quickly as it had arrived. James and Lia didn't know what to make of it.

With the dampness increasing—bringing chilling temperatures that lingered close to the ground—James quickly moved their location back into the woods by the marina's front entrance, further away from the water. Carefully placing Lia on a large tractor tire, James held her close to his chest. Tucking Lia's face into his neck helped with her chattering teeth.

But then, Lia felt James stiffen, and his empathic ability flung outward in an aggressive wave.

James? What is it? Lia sent through their internal link.

More men are approaching at a fast pace. They are in the surrounding area of the field just inland of the marina's road entrance. I sense at least six of them. Their minds are... shielded.

James eased away from Lia and stood up, his gaze fixed on hers.

I'll let my brothers know and find us a place to get out of the way.

Lia rose to stand before him. She grabbed onto his jacket tightly sending him an urgent plea. *But... we need to help them. You... can help them.*

James pulled back and shook her gently. *Honey, I can't risk it. Risk you.*

When you thought earlier that the world needed people like me more, you were wrong, Lia sent that declaration back through their telepathic link. Her hands dropped down, and she stepped away. *The world needs people like you. A warrior who fights for those who can't. A protector who protects what is good in this world.*

James's heart seemed to stop, the weight of his decision pressing down on him. As the path of resolution became clear through Lia's beseeching gaze, he made his move. He stepped up to her, his hands hovering before finally landing on her shoulders.

"I need your help," James whispered, the words hanging in the air.

A hard kiss landed on the top of her head immediately afterward, when James felt her fast-moving nod reply.

James stepped back from her, took in a slow breath, and let it back out with practiced deliberation. All the while, his attention rested on his better half.

Lia met his gaze, and a mirrored firmness of resolve flared brightly in her eyes.

My little warrior, James' gentle voice spoke in her mind.

She nodded back and reached for James' belt loop. "I'm your shadow," Lia whispered back. "Lead the way."

"I'm going to marry you when this is all done," James declared in a barely-there voice.

But Lia heard him loud and clear.

"I know," she replied, tugging on his pants.

James nodded once and then started heading in the direction of his brothers.

Lia gasped, and James spun around swiftly.

Plowing into James' chest, she pushed them further back, gripping his upper arms. "Oh my God!" she whispered harshly.

James grabbed onto Lia, meeting her shocked gaze.

"I—I—think it's my dad!" she said, her voice hoarse from shock.

Frank Marshall eased between the two warriors' readying stances and embraced the older gentleman standing before him. He almost slapped the man's back before thinking better of it.

Stepping back, Frank Marshall met the gaze of a long-lost friend.

"You're holding up well," John Robinson said with warmth and affection. His eyes sparkled with humor before shifting to an expression in keeping with the seriousness of the situation. "Where's my daughter?" he asked sharply.

Josh cleared his throat softly, gaining the stranger's attention. With the similarities in the older man's eye color and facial features, Josh had no difficulty recognizing Lia's father.

"Lia is with my brother, Mr. Robinson. They're staying back until the excitement is over."

John Robinson tilted his head to the side. With his lips pursed, he shook his head in a negative affirmation.

Just then, James sent Josh and Brian an internal message. *I'm coming up to your right. Unfriendlies moving in to surround us.*

"We got incoming," Josh said in a harsh whisper, while swiftly moving John Robinson closer to the large hull of the nearby boat.

Brian tried a similar move on Frank Marshall, but Frank would have none of the younger man's interference.

"Boy, I may not be in the field much anymore, but I'm not helpless."

Already sensing the new arrivals, John Robinson tugged a strange device from his pocket and pressed the tiny switch from its off position to activate.

"Frank, just like old times."

Frank Marshall couldn't help the grin that flashed across his face. "I sure have missed you, John."

James and Lia carefully made their way to the small group. He kept Lia slightly behind him and could feel her vibrating with tension the closer they got to the meeting place.

He could also sense the new enemies getting closer—enemies that had flashed into being all at once from out of nowhere. James found this very strange and concerning.

Coming around a cluster of saplings on the edge of the shipyard, James paused when a strange sensation began to coat his mind. Someone with a powerful presence was probing his mind, filtering through his tightly guarded shields.

His curiosity only intensified when a familiar signature came through the psychic connection. It was similar to how he and his siblings could identify each other, but this new link reminded him of Lia.

It is... my father', Lia confirmed, solidifying what James had already figured out.

James also felt the instant when the intruder touched on the psychic link that led back to his daughter. He felt the immediate realization from John Robinson as he concluded what that link back to Lia truly meant.

Immediately attempting to shield Lia from any repercussions, James gently evicted her from his mind and braced himself.

An icy-hot prickling wave began coating his mind. The strain of keeping his shields up and protecting Lia from the entity's probing caused a piercing ache in his head. Bright red drops began flowing from his nose, and a groan escaped his lips.

Lia growled while swiftly pushing through a rusty link not used in years. She immediately felt the warmth of familiar affection flood her mind. It felt terrific after not feeling his presence in her mind for so long.

Dad! Lia sent through their private connection. *Please ease up on James! He is not used to his power yet. You're hurting him.*

Lia grasped James' shirt and spun him around to face her. She swiped at the blood flowing down his chin and lower lip. She bit down on her lower lip as her eyes reflected sadness for his pain.

James felt relief when the mighty force slowly receded from his mind. He had never felt power like that before. Even the combination of all those previous sources' emotions didn't pack a punch quite like Lia's father.

Carefully easing Lia behind him again, James endeavored to get to his brothers.

The eldest Patterson brother sent Josh and Brian a message as he silently came upon the cluster of old boats on boat jacks. *Unfriendlies coming our way, and I can't sense our men by the front gate.*

James came around the side of the nearest hull, tucking Lia close to the chipped and peeling fiberglass surface while he leaned out to peer around the edge. He could barely make out four silhouettes hiding near the next boat over.

Bolting around James, Lia jumped onto one of the shapes standing in the group. She didn't make a sound, but her body trembled as she held tightly to her father.

Baby girl. Oh, how I've missed you! The voice coated her mind like warm honey.

Lia felt her father gently ease her aside, ensuring she was protected within the circle of men.

Frank Marshall took hold of Lia's shoulders and turned them toward the wooden ladder leaning against the back of the boat. Josh quietly eased Lia up to the first rung.

Bracing her body in stiff resistance, Lia shook her head from side to side. "I'm not leaving James!" she whispered.

James approached her and gently pushed her up to the next ladder's rung, urging her on. "You will help me with the close proximity. I won't go far." Turning to face Josh, he said, "They're coming in hot. We need to find cover and take them out."

Frank Marshall turned toward John Robinson and asked softly, "You going in?"

Chapter Twenty-Nine

J ohn Robinson's head bobbed with urgency. "I'll create a diversion. But be cautious of those men; they're after me, and I can't predict their actions toward others." The urgency in his voice was palpable, setting the scene for the impending danger.

"Dad!" Lia's soft cry, a barely-there whisper, came from just above them.

John, his eyes ablaze with determination, looked up toward the source of the sound. All he could see was a faint silhouette of Lia as she ascended. He turned to his best friend, his voice filled with a father's love and concern. "You keep her safe. Be wary of the incoming team. There are powerful forces at play here." His determination was unshakeable, a testament to his commitment to his daughter and his cause.

Frank took his friend's shoulder in a steadying grasp. "I'm not without some strong forces myself." Marshall jerked his chin once toward his team of warriors, a group of battle-hardened men with scars that told stories of their own. "I got Lia. You boys get going."

Approaching the ladder, Frank reached up to grasp the higher rung. His foot stepped on the lower rung, and his eyes clashed with James'.

James saw the glint of a warrior's battle cry mirrored in Frank Marshall's eyes. As Frank climbed up, the darkness quickly swallowed him as James waited.

"Clear," a voice said softly above.

James tilted the ladder off the boat's deck surface and—with Frank's help above—fed it up to the boat's deck surface above, their movements swift and coordinated.

Turning to his brother, Josh, James gestured to him, indicating he still saw Josh taking the lead. With a swift nod, Josh issued clear instructions, his voice firm and strategic. "I'll circle back to the east and drop behind. Once I've cleared them, I'll flank their rear and provide you with updates."

Josh locked his gaze on the blood still coming from James' nose. Swiveling on the soles of his boots, he met Brian's study. Josh sent out what he wanted them to do through their internal link. Both brothers nodded in understanding and separated quickly.

John Robinson stepped into James' path, blocking his exit. "Frank has told me a lot about you and your brothers. Good stuff. I know my girl is in good hands. Take care of yourself out there." He raised his hand and grasped the back of James' neck.

A piercing shot of hot energy slammed into James' mind. A powerful force surrounded James' shields, providing another layer of protection. The strain James had been operating under since acquiring the empathic gift vanished, leaving him with a profound sense of relief and comfort.

James' mind became quiet once more.

"That should help you out. Protect my daughter, son," John Robinson ordered while backing up in the direction of the mechanical workshop. As he continued walking backward, the swirling wet air, a mix of mist and rain, moved and surrounded him. Soon, John's form was lost in the mist.

Palming his gun, James looked up toward the back of the boat. He prayed Lia would remain safe. His resolve to protect her, and his unwavering commitment and concern for her safety, remained steady.

With his newly gained control over his shields, James could now extend his energy outward, sensing the cold emotions of the approaching enemy. His transformation into a mentally centered soldier was evident in his shifted stance and leveled shoulders. He was ready for the hunt, empowered by his newfound abilities.

A few moments later, John slowly approached Suarez's men standing outside on the wood-planked platform by the industrial sliding doors. His hands were raised high, palms facing outward.

He sensed the men's tension like a thick veil of vibrations crawling along the base of his skull. Figuring it wouldn't help matters if these trigger-happy, nervous ninnies shot him, he sent a wave of calmness to engulf them.

Using the device in his pocket, he transmitted and magnified his power and influence over others' emotions. John stood silently, just within the glow of the lamppost.

He cleared his throat softly when he saw the men relax through various physical cues, and his empathic ability confirmed it.

"I believe you're expecting me," John said calmly, his voice carrying a hint of confidence. His foot rose to rest on the bottom tread, his posture exuding a casual indifference even in the face of danger.

Turning around, the guards faced the direction where John's voice drifted out to them. They spotted the older gentleman at the platform steps. The taller of the two men straightened his shoulders and puffed out his chest. He turned slightly to the man to his right and said, "Tell Suarez his guest has arrived."

Having delivered his command, the taller man pivoted back toward John. His voice was a low growl. "You were supposed to be bringing something with you." The guard descended the steps with deliberate slowness, his gun hanging ominously at his side. Halting just above John, he raised his rifle and jerked it twice to the side. "Step back and turn around," he barked, the tension in the air palpable.

John, with his hands still raised, did as ordered. He stood patiently waiting as the guard patted him down. The device, the size of a miniature garage door opener, sat tucked in John's front pocket. Before Suarez's leading man could find it, he unleashed a powerful wave of energy.

The man took a deep breath and let it out slowly. His shoulders slumped down, and his cares just drifted away. He glanced at John's back before tucking his gun into the small of his back. "Wait here," the guard said, but didn't wait to see if John obeyed his order.

Instead, as John turned slowly around, he watched the guard shrug his shoulders and heave a loud sigh. Stepping around John and the railing post, Suarez's soldier headed toward the side of the outbuilding. The need for downtime away from everything coated his mind and sent him on a quest to find both.

Shifting his focus from the guard, John turned back and sent a wave of urgency toward the occupants inside the machine shop. If the Patterson brothers failed, the men coming for him would be here any moment now, and he needed to be ready.

James' empathic ability was a lifeline, connecting him to his two brothers. He shared all the information his empathic ability could ferret out, keeping them in the loop and united in their mission.

Josh, a master of stealth, seamlessly merged with the surroundings. The fog was no match for his cloaking ability. His skin could mimic any texture or color, and his movements were in perfect harmony with the living nature surrounding them. He was a ghost to the human eye. The only thing keeping Josh slightly discernible, if one looked hard enough, was the choice of clothing he currently donned. Because of the camouflaged khaki pants and shirt, he was careful not to stand by any of the starkly white boat hulls.

Guided by James, Brian's execution was a dance of precision. He flanked the intruders from the rear, his approach swift and calculated. His unique form of telepathy allowed him to absorb the men's fighting patterns, identifying the weakest link. He altered his trajectory. With the stillness of the night surrounding him, Brian closed in on his target, every move a step closer to victory.

With stealthy precision, Brian came up behind the vulnerable man at the back of the formation. Pulling away from the large tree as the tall and heavy-built silhouette eased by his location, he swiftly reached out and wrapped his arm around the man's neck.

Having this hold cut off his airway, the enemy pushed back. The intruder thrust and bucked with all his might to try to off-balance his attacker. But Brian's footing was practiced and ready for these counter maneuvers. Within moments, the stranger's frame went limp and slumped against Brian's chest.

One down. Went out through his internal link to Josh and James.

James responded. *Copy.*

Josh's same response followed, but he added shortly afterward, *Fast-approaching intruders heading toward Frank and Lia's location.*

Switching his direction to intercept, James replied, *Copy—on it.*

A few moments later, he made his way toward the men who had just passed the tire stack where Lia had sat earlier.

Agreeing with Josh's earlier orders and knowing they would disable the targets if possible, James gave these men a chance at surviving. Frank Marshall and his soldiers needed to know about these new arrivals and who had sent them there.

Having some questions of his own, James required answers. Their enemy's focus on Lia's father brought heavy concerns circling back to Lia. If they were after her father, what did that mean for Lia?

For James, there was only one priority—Lia's safety. The thought of her being in danger fueled his determination, making it clear that he would stop at nothing to ensure she was out of harm's way.

Chapter Thirty

L ia shuffled her position for the hundredth time. Feeling carefully along the path of the cockpit benching in front of the swimming platform, she found the vinyl flap of the shrink-wrapped, blue vinyl cocoon.

Frank Marshall, Lia's godfather, spoke softly, "Lia, honey." He positioned his body close to the steering helm, blocking anyone's path toward Lia. He could barely distinguish Lia's slim frame by the dim glow shining through the nearest porthole-shaped clear-vinyl window. These vinyl openings aligned every few yards on the sunk-in cockpit's east and west sides. The outside perimeter lighting cast a blue haze into the metal-framed pocket enclosure up on the boat's deck.

Lia pressed her fingers onto the clear coating at the window. It felt cold against her fingers. She couldn't make out anything past the glow of the perimeter exterior pole lighting. The pocket of lights filtered through the prism of the cloud particles, highlighting a bubble of soupy mist at each light source. The eerie mist, combined with the dim glow of the perimeter lighting, created a sense of foreboding that hung heavily in the air.

"Lia, don't stand in front of the window, honey. Stay to the side." Frank watched as Lia moved and did as he told her.

"I wish this fog would clear up," she said softly.

"I'm sorry I lied about your dad," Frank spoke into the stillness that weighed heavily between them. This tangible tension showed the strain in their relationship.

Lia turned and squinted her eyes, trying to make out Frank through the darkened interior. It was of little use; the small halos of light near the windows couldn't pierce the blue-black void.

But Lia had other senses to count on, which absorbed the warmth of genuine affection from her godfather's mind to hers. *Yes, he did lie to me. But he must have had a hell of a good reason,* she reasoned to herself.

"My dad obviously knew what he was doing. I assume he left for our protection. You were tasked with keeping us safe." Lia's voice, though holding a cold logic, couldn't conceal the hurt and confusion that simmered underneath.

"It was never a task. It was an honor," Frank whispered back.

"Why didn't you just tell us?" Lia wondered softly.

"Everyone needed to believe the explosion killed him. That was the only way you and Michelle could be safe," Frank said with a steely conviction, referring to a past event—a terrorist attack that had shaken their lives. "Plus, there was more than just your lives at stake. Your father made a noble sacrifice to help his people. He never thought it would take so long to accomplish his task."

Lia turned around quietly and jostled the lines at the main winch, and boom. Metal clanked against fiberglass before Lia could grab the lines and fasteners. Their high-pitched screeching sounded harsh in the space around them.

"Why not tell me the extent to which you took, erasing my life from everything?" Lia sighed, not fully understanding the complexity of her situation.

"Because, if you knew what lengths were required, it would bring questions to the surface that I couldn't reveal and leave you open to individuals that could access those thoughts through telepathic means. Or worse. Physical torture."

"What is going on?" Lia harshly whispered.

Her only recollection of her father's work was of an absentminded scientist who loved writing out physics equations at home while calling out answers on Jeopardy.

"Lia, I can't give you that answer. There are so many lives at stake. Yours, your mother's, your dad's, my wife's, and others that I care deeply about. Once you know the answer to that billion-dollar question, you are all in, and there is no going back.

And you're not ready. You're just going to have to trust me on this one. Plus, your father doesn't want you to be involved. Yet."

Yet? Lia wondered how deep this secret went. She opened her mouth to ask just that, but something caught her attention.

A dark blob of movement, barely discernible through the filtering light outside, had Lia getting closer to the cut-out opening. "Someone's coming..." Lia whispered, desperately trying to position the loose lines and deck gear away from her.

Her body suddenly became rigid at the sound of crushed dry leaves and sticks, with the pittering of loose pebbles being kicked up as whoever got closer.

Her head tilted, and Lia swiftly turned, walking a few steps to Frank. She moved forward with her hands out in front of her until her fingers pressed up against Frank's chest. She grabbed and held onto the fabric of his shirt.

Lia's voice was low, under her breath: "It's Mom."

Frank shifted, spun around, and reached for the ladder, which was on its side against the lifeline's starboard deck passage. With Lia's help in keeping the door-like flap held to the side, he got out onto the swim platform and lowered the ladder to the ground. Swiftly and silently, Frank got to the ground and waited close to the boat's hull. When Michelle Robinson reached the ladder's edge, he grabbed her arm and yanked her close to the boat's side.

Frank stifled her harsh gasp with his hand over Michelle's mouth.

At the same time, Lia made her way down and joined them. She pressed her hand onto her mother's arm and leaned into her body. "It's me," Lia whispered into her mother's ear.

Michelle shook her head quickly up and down.

Frank eased off his hand and stepped further back.

When Michelle noticed Frank, she frowned, stepped back, and pulled Lia further away.

"You!" she growled.

"Mom!" Lia harshly whispered, her determination to protect her mother burning in her voice. "You have to let this go for now." Lia tugged on her mother's arm, redirecting her attention back to herself.

Michelle turned toward Lia and raised her palm to Lia's cheek. "Honey, I'm so glad you're okay." She glanced at Frank and then back at her daughter, her relief palpable.

Lia sent waves of calmness into her mother's mind. She also flooded her mother's mind with acceptance and sympathy. When she watched Michelle's face soften and her body ease into a less stiff posture, she eased back. "Mom, how did you get here?"

"Seriously, I wasn't about to stay locked on that aircraft when my husband and daughter needed me." Michelle's voice was filled with defiance as she shot Frank Marshall a look of contempt, then softened her expression for Lia.

"I managed to subdue the charming young man," Michelle said, her voice tinged with sarcasm. She quickly turned back to Frank when she heard his low growl. "He's fine. Just sleeping," she added while holding up a slim syringe in her hand. "I had two left from the stash in your bag. I taped them to my leg. No one bothered to search my person." She glared a fierce look toward Frank.

Lia pulled her mother's arm and swiped the syringe from her hand. "How did you find us?"

Michelle smiled and yanked on Lia's jacket. "I put a bug in your jacket's pocket. I installed an app on my phone to track it." Her resourcefulness was evident in every action she took, leaving Frank grudgingly impressed.

"Didn't my men take your phone?" Frank asked with a low growl.

"I cloned my phone and kept it taped to my lower back. Like I said before, no one searched my body," Michelle said, a sly smile creeping onto her face. "Really, Frank, you are all amateurs."

"Mother!" Lia reprimanded, her concern for the situation evident in her tone. "You're not helping!"

"Yes, I am, dear," Lia's mother replied as she folded her arms against her chest and tapped her foot on the ground. "The first step to fixing a problem is to know about it." She raised her hands, gesturing toward Frank. "I'm letting him know."

Lia sighed loudly as her head moved from side to side.

Frank also felt the need to release a heavy sigh before saying, "Why didn't I listen to Jenna when I had the chance?"

Michelle swiveled and pointed one finger at Frank's chest. "You should always listen to Jenna. She is a delightful woman and way too good for the likes of you!"

Reaching for Michelle's arm, Frank gently dragged her toward the ladder.

Michelle braced her hands on either side of the ladder's rails and pushed her body away. She shook her head rapidly from side to side, making her objection known.

Frank began turning her around to hoist her up into a fireman's hold when the crack of a gunshot exploded in the distance.

James had been studying the emblem on the pocket of the enemy's all-dark-gray jumpsuit. After securing the man with zip ties and duct tape across his mouth, James dragged his unconscious prisoner to the littered stack of industrial-sized tires. The man's partner had already been bound and tucked in place just moments before.

James' body froze when the sound of two shots fired ripped through the surrounding area.

He tilted his head and remained still, sending a telepathic message.

Lia, are you okay, honey?

James, come quick. My mom's with me, Lia replied.

The direction of the gunshots had gotten muffled and distorted in the mist. James couldn't be sure, but it sounded close to the water's edge by the outbuildings, not near Lia and Frank.

James cursed under his breath before taking one last look at the men leaning against a stack of tires. After ensuring his measures for securing them would have to do, James quickly returned to Lia, Frank, and now... Michelle Robinson.

Chapter Thirty-One

Just moments before:

John Robinson didn't waste a moment when Suarez and his two men emerged to stand by the workshop's dock platform, just short of the steps. He directed a fresh wave of hostility toward the traitor in Suarez's team, and the tension between them increased tenfold.

The pale-haired man, who had gone inside to announce John's arrival, was ready to proceed with Herrera's cutthroat orders. John's arrival gave him the signal to unleash the violence that had been brewing within him.

Suarez looked around, just noticing his other 'man's disappearance. He shook his head, his jaw clenching tightly. A frown moved across Suarez's face as he turned toward his remaining men before switching his gaze onto John Robinson. "I had my doubts you would come," he said softly.

"You had my wife and daughter. You left me no choice." John's hands slid into his front pockets, his body language a mix of resignation and anger. "Can I trust you to release them?" he asked, the sense of betrayal heavy in his voice.

The politician's smile held all the assurances of that profession. The words that followed held no ounce of truth. "You have my word. Just as soon as you hand over the sol-fusion energy source."

John nodded and gestured toward the edge of the property, where the dense woods began. "Do you want me to take you to it? It's just beyond those trees."

Suarez swiveled and gestured toward the man at his side. With an arm swinging up and hand waving toward John, Suarez motioned for the newly hired security man to go before him.

The 'traitor's gaze fixed on John Robinson as he slowly backed away from the group. Before returning to Suarez, his eyes slowly traced a path from John to the other security man. When the gaze connected with Suarez, it hardened. The tightness around his eyes and the clenching of his jaw were the only warning Suarez received before a gun was pointed at him.

No chance stood for expletive shouts to blast from Suarez's mind to his tongue and lips.

Herrera's man pressed the weapon's trigger, and the gun went off in two explosive bangs.

In the wooded area of the marina's property line to the north, Josh Patterson stepped back and stood still instantly. Tilting his head to the side, he waited for more gunfire while quickly checking in with his brothers.

Once he received the 'all clear' from them both, he hastily snapped a photo on his cell phone of the two faces of the knocked-out soldiers. He hesitated briefly before leaning forward again, this time to capture a quick image of the woman's high-tech jumpsuit's graphic logo.

The woman's face drew his gaze again. A black fastener held her dark, blue-black hair up into a high ponytail. His eyes traced a path from her forehead to her elegant jawline. Josh couldn't stop the accelerated beat of his heart. There would likely be a bruise on the delicate-looking face.

A neutral expression replaced the closed eyes and clenched jaw. A glint of coldness entered the pooling depths of the second eldest 'brother's eyes. He released a long exhale.

Looks were definitely deceiving; the woman may have looked tiny and fragile, but she carried a hard left hook and a mean rear-axe kick. Josh rubbed his chin and jaw. He would have a few bruises, too.

Shaking his head, he turned away from the urge to study her longer. After the mission's completion, they'd get one of the men to gather the prisoners and take them back to headquarters. He'd have a chance to question her then.

He pocketed his device after checking in and sending a quick update: *Two more down.* He sent telepathically to both Brian and James.

Josh received a response back from Brian: *Three more targets neutralized.* Meanwhile, James' intel let them know there were still two more out there.

The hunt was still on, and time was wasting.

Michelle Robinson spun around and headed toward the dock's outbuildings.

Frank Marshall caught her just in time before she could lose them in the fog and barrel into God knows what kind of trouble.

"Let go of me!" Michelle whispered harshly while struggling to get away. From the tightness of his hold, her arms would likely have bruising.

Rushing forward, Lia grabbed onto the fisted grasp of her mother's jacket. "Mom, going out there will only make matters worse."

"Lia! Your father needs my help!" Michelle's voice, filled with frantic determination, continued to shift and pull from Frank's gripping hold.

Suddenly, James emerged from behind the group and embraced Lia and her mother.

He looked toward Frank and jerked his chin in concise, small movements.

Frank immediately let go of Michelle's arms.

Michelle burrowed into her daughter's hair. She whimpered in frustration, wanting to reach her husband. Her body vibrated with the need to move.

James' voice was calm and strategic as he brought his lips close to Lia's and Michelle's ears. "'You've got to remain quiet. There are two more assailants on the south end of the property. Sound will travel along the edge of the water. They may not know in which direction to get to us, but they'll know we're out here. Keeping our presence hidden gives us the only advantage."

Lia quickly nodded her head up and down. After several seconds passed, Michelle, much slower, did the same.

James stepped back.

Michelle moved away from Lia and let her gaze clash with James'. Nodding again, she brought her arms around her upper chest.

Stilling, James felt a wisp of cold emotion coating his mind.

Swiftly pulling Lia and her mother to the side of the sailboat's hull, he prompted them to kneel close to the massive metal keel. He held his hands out with the palms pointed downward, bouncing them in the air as a signal for them to stay low and stay put.

Frank Marshall brought his gun out front and systematically searched the surrounding boats.

James eased his way next to Frank. Using his free hand, he communicated through their silent sign language—understood only by team members—a testament to their seamless teamwork.

Nodding, with his back against the fiberglass hull, Frank made his way in the direction James indicated.

Stalking with careful steps, James moved to the east side of the boatyard. The cold, prickling sensation from the nearest assailant guided James to intercept.

With Frank falling back to loop behind, they would have the enemy surrounded.

Back by the machine's workshop, the gun that had fired two lethal shots stayed primed in the pale-haired man's hand.

A rattling of metal hitting against the dock's structure vibrated around them. Suarez's body hitting the water made the floating dock rock up and down. The sudden movement of the water slapped against the nearby pylons, then ricocheted off the dock's retaining wall before landing.

Herrera's traitor jerked the gun in two quick successions toward John Robinson's chest. With a smirk and gleeful gleam in his eyes, the young man felt no remorse for the two lives lost by his hand.

Never breaking eye contact with the one holding the gun on him, John slowly stepped back from the steps. The other now-lifeless body had fallen down the platform steps and landed on the ground by John's booted feet.

John eased back the aggressive suggestions he sent telepathically and replaced them with soothing waves of calmness. Slowly bringing his hands up, palms facing outward, leveled with his shoulders, John said, "I take it there's been a change of plans?"

The gun's position twitched to the side again. "Nice and easy. You are going to take me to this invention of yours."

At the opposite end of the marina, with a faint snap of a tree branch, the intruder approached the salvaged carcass of the abandoned tugboat. The moon peeked out from the passing clouds, casting long shadows against the hulking maritime giants captured and discarded on land.

James pulled away from the nearby boat's jack support and got ready.

The bulge of the heavily muscled man's tread fell solidly on the ground with every step. Stealth obviously wasn't the assailant's concern at the moment, which was worrisome to James.

James barely felt the icy-hot trickle of anticipation coming from the approaching person's mind before the man came up from behind.

The enemy suddenly turned around and kicked out, expecting to hit James' lower thigh with a brutal sweep.

But that didn't happen. James, with his extraordinary agility and the power of telekinesis, flipped back. He sprang his body in a fluid backflip that quickly countered the assailant's attack, positioning himself a few feet away.

James again felt that rush of eagerness coming from the other man's mind before the enemy quickly engaged in hand-to-hand combat that resembled something between Defendu and Krav Maga. An undercurrent of satisfaction immersed the man's every aggressive movement.

Knowing there wasn't much time before company showed up, James swept his hand out and sent a wave of telekinetic energy at his opponent.

The man flew back into the air, slamming into the nearest boat's side. But amazingly enough, the hit didn't take him down—a testament to his resilience that added to the challenge James faced.

James' foe landed on his feet, shook off the hit, and got into a bracing stance.

Hands raised and fingers cupped toward his palms, the man sent James a hand gesture. With his palms facing up, the man moved his fingers, repetitively tapping against each palm. *Bring it on*, it silently said.

James witnessed a different result when he sent out another telekinetic sweep of power. The wave of energy bounced off a shield surrounding his opponent in a four-foot circumference.

A smirk appeared around the enemy's mouth. He flexed his shoulders and arms and fisted his hands before striding toward James' location.

Realizing this would have to be done the hard way, James let out a loud, disgruntled sigh. Fisting his hands, he stalked toward the incoming threat. He couldn't afford the sound of gunfire or objects crashing around to notify his position to other intruders.

Taking advantage of Lia's attention on James and the enemy, Michelle carefully crept back and tucked close to the hull's fiberglass surface.

Before Lia could stop her, a fleeting movement came and went. Michelle, focused on her footing around obstacles, hurried to meet up with her husband, her every step adding to the dangerous outcome of the unfolding situation.

Chapter Thirty-Two

J ohn Robinson led Herrera's man to the edge of the marina's property, where the wooded area met the dock's water's edge. A large shape, the size of a plastic storage tub, sat on the ground. The object had a black, shiny canvas shielding its rounded shape from view.

Herrera's man quickly threw the covering off onto the ground nearby. What stood before them was a complicated shape of cylinders, angled pieces, tubes, wires, tanks, and louvers that came together in a disjointed series of fused parts.

"What the hell is it?" the man said with reluctant awe.

"An energy source of mysterious origin, capable of powering a large city off the grid," John said softly, bringing more questions than answers to Herrera's lackey's mind.

The man switched his fascination from the convoluted shape to meet John's eyes before glancing around the area. "How did you get this thing here?"

Letting a small smile form on his face, John answered, "Well, that's an interesting story..."

The gun tilted, left to right, a few times as John's explanation stalled. "Yeah?" the gunman prompted, hoping to give John a reason to continue.

But that wasn't the result. Instead, John's attention flashed just beyond Herrera's lackey's shoulder.

With that subtle warning, the gunman's body sprang into motion.

However, his actions did no good. Before Herrera's lackey could even complete the turn, Josh Patterson had him disarmed and subdued with a swift blow to the head.

Catching the slumped body, Josh dragged the enemy off to the side and swiftly bound his hands and feet.

"That's quick work there, son," John said while picking up the canvas sheet and reapplying it over the mechanical device. Although this piece replicated an earlier version that would simulate the actual fusion device and appease those who wanted it, John didn't want any parts of this technology landing in the wrong hands if he could help it.

After covering the fake, John turned and met Josh's serious expression. "Let's get back to Frank. I have a few minutes to say goodbye to Lia before I go."

Michelle Robinson, her heart pounding, hurried away from the boatyard's graveyard of discarded ships, sailboats, barges, and towers of stacked dinghies. With the moon hidden once again by clouds, she lost the advantage of its illumination, heightening the sense of urgency.

Stumbling, her foot snagged on a winching rope, causing her to trip and get caught on one of the massive boat jacks. Pulling the tangled line away from her foot, Michelle paused when she heard some stones hitting the ground coming up behind her.

Michelle hurriedly pushed off the metal structure and ran into the clearing before the docks. With the sound of someone approaching closer, she turned back and squinted her eyes, following a trail around the last of the boats.

Just past the last boat-jack, Lia, in a surprising turn of events, hurriedly approached, unleashing a wave of telekinetic energy in a frantic bid to stop her mother. The result was a whirlwind of debris and an unintended consequence: a forceful push that sent Michelle Robinson crashing to the ground, her yelp a mix of surprise and pain.

Racing to her mother's side, Lia helped her to rise.

"You shouldn't have followed me. Lia, go back this instant," Michelle ordered, her voice filled with determination as she brushed off the sand and dirt from her clothes.

Swiftly shaking her head from side to side, Lia said, "Come back with me." She caught onto her mother's arm, urging Michelle back toward Frank and James.

An abstract shape separated from the shadows beneath the workshop's overhang—footsteps on a raised platform vibrated against the wood planks.

Amado Herrera stood at the top of the workshop's platform with a gun, pointing in their direction. "Actually, ladies, you're both staying put." He raised his voice to carry through the deep fog that enveloped the surrounding marina. The gun was cocked and pointed toward Lia.

He tilted his head to the side and waited a few seconds before raising his voice again. "If you want the women to remain unharmed, you all should make your way back to the shipyard's workshop."

Herrera escaping custody hadn't played into anyone's plan, and the advantage swiftly changed hands.

James was still fighting his attacker when Herrera voiced the threat. Lia's terror flooded his mind in a numbing chill, making him hesitate. But he saved himself at the last minute, narrowly avoiding a kick to the head that would have knocked him to the ground.

Jumping back to avoid the kick, James spotted Frank Marshall making his way around the broken shell of the tugboat. Frank tilted his head to the side and raised his gun.

James' choices narrowed to one thing: keeping their position guarded no longer mattered. He lashed out in a series of wide-swinging kicks that pushed the other man back toward the tugboat.

A shot rang out, and James' assailant fell backward to the ground. With a snarled groan, the man held the back of his thigh.

Frank and James swiftly approached the fallen foe from opposite sides. As James grabbed the man's hands to bind him, Frank did the same for his legs. In a flash, they had their prisoner secured.

James ripped off a length of duct tape and covered the man's mouth.

Frank tore the fabric around the wound and quickly checked the man's thigh. Seeing that the bullet had gone clean through, Frank tore away the rest of the pant leg and wrapped the cloth like a bandage around the wound.

With another rip, James wrapped the length of duct tape around Frank's application. When the wound looked secure, James and Frank each took an arm of the prisoner and dragged him up against the side of the nearest boat.

Lia heard the gunshot and flinched, but James' telepathic message calmed her panic and kept a tethered link on her fleeting telekinetic control.

We're good. On our way to you.

Okay. I'll wait for your signal. Lia sent back to James.

Herrera cleared his throat and stepped back from the top step. His gaze skimmed the area around him. Two jerks on the gun were the only indication Herrera gave while easing slowly backward. Pivoting the gun to the side, he pointed to the sidewall of the workshop's one-story addition that protruded from the three-story main building.

Lia clasped her mother's arm and gave a slight squeeze.

Michelle slowly nodded back.

While leaning against the main building's exterior wall, he watched as Lia and her mother made their way up the steps. He smiled when Lia jolted suddenly upon spotting the dead man at the bottom of the platform.

The body's position made navigating the steps tricky. With little clearance available in lengths matching the capabilities of each woman's stride, and the body blocking most of the handrail, the trek up to the next level without falling into the water became a complicated feat. Carefully finding her footing around the body on the ground, Lia led the way up the steps, with her mother slowly following behind.

As the two women headed to the area indicated, Herrera switched his gaze to the cloudy mist of the surrounding dock area.

A jostling of pebbles had his attention darting to the left.

John Robinson and Josh Patterson stepped out from the adjacent one-story outbuilding. With their hands both raised in surrender, they slowly walked toward the dock's edge.

When Michelle Robinson spotted her husband, she jerked and started toward him.

Herrera's quick order of, "Don't even think about it," made Michelle freeze in place.

Tugging on her mother's arm, Lia pulled her along the sidewall. With their backs against the shiplap surface, the women watched as the new arrivals made their way closer.

Lia grimaced at the tight squeeze her mother had on her hand with each step the men took toward them.

"Glad you could make it, John," Herrera sneered disdainfully. "Now, all we're missing is the other Patterson brothers."

Herrera's gaze zeroed in on Josh Patterson's cold stare.

"You're down to just three," he boasted.

Josh's jaw tightened at the cruel, jabbing remark about Sean, but he remained quiet.

Brian Patterson stepped around the one-story building near the east side of the docks. The same outbuilding that housed the main office and store where Lia and Frank were first held. Raising his hands slowly in surrender, Brian carefully headed toward their group.

Herrera saw movement out of the corner of his eye. He quickly lunged toward the women and wrenched Lia's arm.

Yanking her to his chest, he backed up to a more advantageous position. With Lia pressed against his front, he thought she provided a perfect shield. Plus, the gun shoved up against the side of her skull added another guarantee against any aggressive attacks.

"Everyone needs to move slowly," Herrera said, tilting his head to the side and glaring at Michelle Robinson with hatred. "Martha-fucking-Stewart, against the wall. Any sudden movements, and my trigger finger will get twitchy." His gaze bounced between each approaching man.

Brian nodded slowly. Exiting the floating pier, he made his way up to a higher level on the ramp connecting both shipyard areas.

John Robinson's gaze landed on his wife. He calmly followed Brian up to the higher area, never breaking contact with Michelle.

Michelle's gaze darted between her husband and her daughter as her hands tightly grasped together.

When John came to stand beside her, she reached out a hand and anchored herself to him.

John instantly sent soothing waves of calmness to his wife and toward Lia.

Brian watched as Josh came up the side steps to stand beside him.

A scattering of pebbles kicked notified the group that an approaching visitor was on their way.

All too soon, Lia watched as Frank Marshall's form began to solidify from the surrounding darkness. His movements stayed slow and steady.

"Where's James Patterson?" Herrera asked.

"He's locked in a battle with someone who, I don't think, works for either of our governments." Frank carefully reached the step platform and leaned forward to rest on the guardrail. His gaze searched Herrera's face before speaking again. "What do you hope to accomplish here tonight?" Frank asked with quiet authority.

"I want John Robinson, his invention, and you to come along quietly," Herrera divulged with arrogant confidence. The barrel of his gun pressed into Lia's forehead, and he took sadistic pleasure in hearing her whimper. "Or Lia and Michelle will pay the consequences."

Frank slowly nodded his head. "Okay," he said softly, shifting his gaze to Lia and Michelle. He added, "Let them go, and we'll come with you."

Chapter Thirty-Three

"Do you really take me for a fool?" Herrera screamed, and spittle sprung from his mouth. His eyes flashed to Michelle Robinson. "Slowly pull out your pockets!" he ordered.

Michelle dropped her husband's hand and did as he said.

"Inside-out, one at a time," Herrera further instructed.

Michelle did the first pocket, the side by her husband. A cell phone dropped out and landed on the dock's wooden surface.

The second pocket revealed two syringes. Before they could drop to the ground, Herrera yelled out, "Keep a hold of them!"

When Michelle wrapped her hand around the needles, Herrera nodded his head up and down. Pleased that his calculations on Michelle Robinson's persistence stood correct, he allowed his plan to unfold.

"I want you to use the drug on the Patterson brothers—"

No one moved for several heartbeats, and this pushed Herrera over the edge. He shouted, "Now!" His voice rang in Lia's ear as he snapped her back tighter to his chest. The barrel of his gun pressed with more force, causing her to whimper again.

Everything within Lia vibrated with the need to keep a lid on the unpredictable power of the telekinesis ability she received when linking James and her life forces together. No telling what damage could happen if she let that energy out, doing more harm than good.

Tell your mother to do it, James instructed, using their telepathic link and helping to cage in her new telekinesis power. Whatever magic John Robinson extended to him allowed James to master control of both the empathic ability and telekinesis in himself, allowing him to give assistance to Lia as well.

"Mom, please," Lia pleaded. The relief in feeling James' connection anchored her control.

Michelle's nod was quick, her hand trembling around the syringes. She struggled with the cap, and her fingers struggled to perform the simple task. It wasn't nerves that hindered her, but the numbing cold of the water. If not for this physical obstacle, she would have executed the task without hesitation. Her love for her husband and child was the driving force behind her every action.

When the cap finally came off, Michelle turned to Josh Patterson, her face blank, but her eyelids blinked rapidly. She carefully approached the large, towering soldier, instinctively knowing he was the more dangerous foe.

But Josh just nodded to Michelle, making no movements to resist.

She quickly plunged the needle and pressed the end down to administer the drug into his system.

All too quickly, Josh Patterson's large body buckled.

John Robinson caught the young man's frame and grunted. Struggling with Josh's deadweight, he carefully lowered the unconscious man down.

Michelle looked to Herrera in time to see his chin jerk toward Brian Patterson.

"Again!" he shouted.

Nodding again, showing her compliance, she stepped closer to Brian. She tried to do the same with him, but her hands were shaking too much from adrenaline and the dropping temperature. She couldn't get the cap off.

"Let me," Brian said quietly. He gently took the needle from her and flicked off the cap. He pierced the needle in his other arm and pressed down on the plunger. Quickly yanking out the needle, he dropped it. His back slammed against the nearby wall's surface, sliding down the paneling until his butt hit the wooden planks—hard.

As the drug coursed through his system, Brian slumped to the side and fell over.

Herrera smiled with a chilling glee. "The mighty Patterson brothers, so easily conquered."

Turning to Frank, Herrera ordered, "Bind them." His voice lowered to a more normal volume level.

Frank slowly made his way to the closest unconscious man, Josh Patterson. Bending down, he reached for Josh's shoulder. Looking up at Herrera, he explained, "I'll need help getting him turned over. He should have some zip-ties in his back pocket."

Herrera made eye contact with John. "Do it," he said harshly, while yanking Lia harder to him.

Get ready to drop, Lia. James' order came through in harsh, urgent volume through their link.

Lia's body trembled. She hoped her limbs would obey when she needed them to.

John pushed on one side while Frank pulled on Josh's arm. Josh's frame quickly fell on his side.

"Throw his gun in the water!" Herrera yelled when spotting Josh's weapon. He wrenched Lia tight to his body for more protection. "Do it!" he cried louder.

A loud splash broke the silence, evidence that Frank had carried out Herrera's order.

Frank grabbed some ties from Josh's pocket as John pushed Josh onto his stomach. Both of them, working together, got Josh's arms held back and bound.

"Now, the other," Herrera said, his voice sounding more secure.

As Frank went to stand, suddenly a fiery explosion lit up the night nearby. Understanding exactly what that explosion meant, Frank used the distraction to leap to the side, aiming to tackle Herrera.

Herrera was caught off guard, wobbling the gun and loosening his hold on Lia.

Lia instantly dropped to the ground.

Frank plowed into Herrera's center mass before Herrera could grab Lia again. The force of the tackle had Herrera's head hitting the exterior wall.

Dazed from the hit, but not out, Herrera's knees went out. But he still had a hold on his gun.

Frank landed on top and swiftly rolled Herrera to the side.

Lia crawled out from under Herrera's legs as the men struggled for the gun.

John Robinson quickly tugged his daughter to her feet, helping her to stand.

"Go to your mother," he yelled.

James Patterson came barreling up the platform. His gaze stayed steady on Lia. He dragged her to him and hugged her hard. "You scared me to death," he whispered in her ear.

Suddenly, Herrera evaded Frank's hold on his arm. He swung the gun around and aimed toward the couple as they embraced.

With a shout of warning, Michelle Robinson bolted forward as the gun went off.

James broke away from Lia, pulling her behind him. When he spun around, he was able to catch Michelle Robinson as she fell.

Frank Marshall caught Herrera's arm and pushed it down to the wood planks with a thundering slam. The impact released the gun from Herrera's hand, but the damage had already been done.

Jumping out from behind James, Lia watched Frank struggle to subdue Herrera, who was fighting back as if demon-possessed. Fearing the worst if Herrera should break free yet again, she leaped down and grabbed onto Herrera's flailing leg. With her touch, waves upon waves of emotional energy came out using her empathic ability. Flooding his psyche with panic, she attacked.

Herrera's eyes widened as he screamed. His features held a grim expression of shock and pain before going slack.

Jumping back, Lia swiftly turned away, unable to look at what she had done. The fact Herrera was no longer a threat to them looped within her thoughts.

James called Lia's name softly. Cradling Michelle Robinson, watching as Michelle's eyes blinked as tears leaked out, obscuring her vision, he felt powerless.

Lia and her father rushed toward Michelle Robinson's collapsed frame.

John quickly gathered Michelle into his arms.

Michelle clasped his arm. Her mouth moved, and John had to lean closer to hear her. "Is our baby okay?" she choked out while swallowing numerous times.

John nodded a couple of times. "Yes, my love. You saved her."

"Good," she sighed and let her eyes close.

"Ahh!" Lia cried while holding onto her mother's hand.

John quickly stood and kept Michelle tight to his chest. Spinning around, he met Frank's gaze. "If I get her to my—"

Frank nodded quickly in understanding. "Of course. Go," he ordered. "I'll get Lia home safely."

Lia's father looked down as James helped Lia to stand. "I'll get her help. She'll be okay..." He hesitated before continuing, "I should've never left her alone. Forgive me," he pleaded. Knowing that his disappearance not only prevented his wife from that constant supply of his powerful empathic ability, but his physical presence was what kept Michelle on the correct course in life. He also realized that his current decision would leave his daughter behind without them both.

"There's nothing to forgive, Daddy." Lia's smile was heartbreaking. "Just take care of Mother."

John nodded and quickly hurried away. "Take care of my daughter," he shouted to Frank and James.

As he rushed away down the steps and toward the woods, the darkness quickly enveloped them, and they soon disappeared from view.

Lia rushed to James.

He enveloped her in his arms and held on tightly.

Frank Marshall cleared his throat and got their attention.

James turned with Lia, not letting her go.

"What happened with the other assailant?" Frank asked.

"I blew him up in the explosion," James said, while his hand pressed Lia's head close to the curve of his neck. Her jerking shakes became more substantial, and James swept her into his arms. He sent soothing waves through their telepathic link, trying to ease back the shock pumping through her system.

Lia's body went slack as she lost consciousness, and James repositioned her in his arms.

"Is she okay?" Frank asked while he checked Herrera's pulse. Finding the pulse in his neck beating strong, he quickly grabbed more of Josh's zip ties.

"Yeah, I sent her to sleep. The shock was—" James started to reply.

A loud humming filled the area around them. The mechanical buzzing was back. That eerie light, along with the growing fog, also returned, reflecting on everything around the remaining group and casting them all in a pale green glow.

James' head tilted up, along with Frank Marshall's. They watched as the globe of the light's sphere got smaller in the sky. When it became a small, bubble-like feature that looked like it could fit in one's hand, the humming noise ceased, and a profound silence enveloped everything.

As if on cue, a few moments later, the fog vanished, revealing the night's stars twinkling in a clear sky.

Chapter Thirty-Four

Lia woke with a start and tried to turn over in the hospital bed, but it was challenging to do so with James' large frame tucked close.

James automatically adjusted his large frame closer to one of the bed rails and eased Lia around.

"Hey, you," her voice whispered as she watched him blink open his eyes.

"Hey, you," he replied in a groggy voice. "How are you feeling?"

"I guess okay." She yawned widely. "Still tired. Don't know why I woke up. Bad dream, maybe."

Lia shifted and got comfortable. Her arms went up around his neck, and she pressed her trembling lips to the opening of his shirt collar—a gesture that revealed her vulnerability in that moment.

James sighed heavily and gathered closer. There were so many things he wanted to say, but the words seemed to escape him. He didn't know where to start.

With their minds in sync, Lia knew what to do. "How about starting with this…" Lia tilted her head up and puckered her lips together.

James smiled and then leaned down. Their lips met in a gentle kiss.

All too soon in Lia's way of thinking, James pulled back from the kiss. He watched Lia's eyes flutter open.

"I love you," he whispered.

"Love you, too," she said but started to pull away.

"Where are you going?" James tugged her back down. His eyes went to the entrance door, and the lock clicked closed, locking them in and keeping everyone else out.

"I thought you'd want to go check on everyone."

Lia's attention went to James' hand as her top slid upward, exposing her stomach and bra. She quickly met James' gaze, and what she saw in his eyes made her heartbeat speed up.

"I almost lost you," James whispered. "Baby, I didn't know I could get that scared."

His touch stroked her soft skin, and his mouth dropped to leave a trail of soft bites and warm, wet caresses. His fingers nimbly released the fasteners on both her bra and jeans.

Giving his full consideration to disposing of the rest of her clothes, James only stopped when her body was naked and on display. His eyes studied everything laid out before him like a gift—taking in all her dips and valleys and the delectable contours of her body.

When Lia's hands went to his T-shirt, James pulled his visual worshipping back onto her face.

"I need you," James spoke softly, and the extent of that need was relayed through their internal connection.

"What about me flinging stuff around?" Lia asked, referring to her lack of telekinetic control.

"I'll be able to lend you a hand with that," James replied smiling, pressing his lips against hers. He still wasn't sure what Lia's father did to him back at the marina. But at the moment, he didn't care.

Lia nodded back accepting his lips and hurriedly pushing at his cotton shirt.

Impatient with her progress, James helped her and quickly removed the rest of the barriers, allowing them to touch skin to skin. His hands shook as they pushed Lia's thighs open to settle between her legs.

"Baby, I can't wait," James implored forgiveness. The need to connect their bodies rode out all other reasoning.

Lia's head moved from side to side. Her fingers grasped the bed linen. Tightly, she held to the fabric, needing an anchor to stay tethered to this moment. But James wanted her to soar, so his fingers parted her folds to set her flying.

He stroked those sensitive bundles of nerves, sending waves of tingling pleasure. Her hips unknowingly raised up and down. Rocking toward that place that James seemed so apt at sending her to, she released the mangled bed sheets and dug her nails into James' lower arms.

"Please. James!"

James felt the wetness coat his fingers and broke off contact. Just as Lia opened her lips to protest, he filled her wanting need once more. With finesse a distant memory, he stroked her core with powerful movements.

Lia shouted out, feeling so full of him. Her muscles tightened all around him.

They both moved erratically together. Their hips slammed in a disjointed rhythm as need pulsed hot, and subtlety was forfeited to bodily and emotional necessity.

James captured Lia's hands, entwined within his as they rushed toward that incandescent pinnacle, and their hearts meshed together—becoming one in both body and soul.

The flash of their climax encapsulated them onto another plane, and time seemed to stop. The bursting of pleasures peaked where their bodies joined and spread outward throughout every nerve-ending. Their bodies remained heated, with sweat beading their skin.

The hot air from the room's heating unit—a relentless assault on their burning flesh—made every tiny hair coating the skin feel brushed from the air's movement. The shivers of their bodies, more a reaction to touch rather than the air's cooler temperature, were a testament to their physical vulnerability. James, in a bid to provide them comfort, reached for the bedding and tossed the light blanket over them.

Only after several moments went by, with their heartbeats returning to normal, did the heat pumping through their veins decrease, and the warmer temperatures of the room's ventilation felt comfortable on their partly exposed limbs once more.

Lia sighed and slowly opened her eyelids. She studied her lover's face and traced one finger around his relaxed lips.

This attention had James smiling, but his eyes remained closed, enjoying the closeness. He wanted to stay in this bubble of contentment for a few more moments.

Of the same mind, Lia let the minutes tick by, wanting this place out of time to regroup. But all too soon, other concerns leaked within. There were things needing their attention and other priorities flooding in. Easing away, pulling herself up, she searched the room as she swung the covers off herself and James.

"I guess we are getting up?" James helped Lia sit fully up and watched as she swung her legs around to the edge of the bed.

Lia sighed and looked around for her clothes. Scattered around the floor by the bed, each article was picked up and quickly donned. James liked watching her put each piece back in place—but not nearly as much as taking them off.

He chuckled when his clothing got chucked at him and took the hint to get into his gear.

As they got dressed, sounds beyond the door made their way to them. The rolling of carts along hard floors, the murmuring of people coming and going, and the buzzing of medical equipment associated with a functioning hospital seeped into their awareness.

James finished putting on his boots as Lia looked for her sneakers.

"They're on the top shelf in the closet," James told her while tying the knot on his footwear. He was partly shirtless, and Lia was sidetracked by his exposed arms and chest. James chuckled again and met her flushed face.

"Hey, don't look at me. I'm not the one who's all fired up to get dressed."

Lia swung away from temptation and quickly walked over to get her shoes. Once retrieved, she sat down on the sofa.

"We need to go check on your brothers. And I know you want to get any updated reports. Plus—"

"All that can wait," James grumbled while buttoning up his shirt. "Seriously, Lia," he added donning his shirt fully, "you need to rest."

"You and I will rest at home…" Lia picked up one of the sneakers and began loosening the shoelaces.

James grinned. "Yeah, baby. Home. I should move in with you right away. After all, you did promise to marry me."

Lia's gaze raised to meet James as he suddenly stood up, reading her thoughts. "Your parents will be with you in spirit, love. When they return, we'll do something formal-like with everyone."

"Formal-like," Lia repeated, her mind swirling with uncertainty. She blew out a loud exhale—a sign of her inner turmoil—and hesitated before leaning down to put on her shoe.

James strode over to her, kneeled, and picked up the other sneaker. Leaning down, he raised her foot and slipped on the white canvas footwear. When the laces were entirely tied, their eyes met.

"I know I'm not the Prince Charming of your dreams, and I'm not that romantic guy in the rom-com movies—"

Lia, pressing her finger on James' lips, interrupted him. "You are everything I dreamed of and more," she whispered. "But… you also said when everything was done. This situation is far from—"

"We are getting married. Today! Or at the latest, tomorrow. Everything else… can wait. I held off long enough to finally meet you—I'm not letting you go for anything." James' voice was firm, his determination palpable as he stood up and reached for Lia's hand.

Lia slowly put her hand in his; with their eyes locked on each other, James pulled her up and clenched her to his chest. He leaned down and spoke in her ear, "Two kids and a dog. That's what you said in Mexico, and I'm not letting you back out."

Lia's smile pressed into James' skin just under his chin. She kissed him on the curve of his neck, her playful tone evident as she mumbled, "How about a dog first? Then the kids are up for debate."

"Deal," James grunted. "Let's go get started."

Epilogue

"I'm fine, damn it!" Josh Patterson grumbled when the nurse entered the hospital room to change his IV saline solution. He had been in a coma lasting all night into early afternoon. His eyes, heavy with sleep, wanted to shut closed again, but he fought the sleepiness like a toddler during naptime.

He wanted to pull out the IV port, but James, his older brother, pushed him back into the reclined position on the bed. They were all concerned because it had taken much longer for Josh to be revived than everyone had counted on.

The sedative got further flushed from Josh's system with every bag that emptied into him. The nurse said it would be at least a couple more bags before it was completely gone from his system.

"Stop being such a big baby," Brian teased, leaning back into the nearby recliner chair. His own bag of saline was tethered to his arm. His eyes, tired but filled with a mischievous glint, met Josh's glare.

Luck would have it, the syringe Michelle Robinson used on Brian hadn't been a full dosage. She had used half of the drug already on the guard left behind with her on the helicopter. So Brian had come around much sooner than Josh.

Josh glared at his younger brother and replied, "Bite me."

"No thanks," Brian chuckled tiredly. "You're probably way too tough and chewy."

Lia wrapped her arm around James' back and hugged him. The contact helped keep everyone in the surrounding area out of James' mind.

Whatever Lia's father did to James had worn off when they came into Josh's room. But it gave James some hope that he could eventually function independently. He would have to work on providing stronger shields around his new gift.

Lia tugged him closer. "Hopefully not as normally as you had in the past." James' previous habit of storming into danger alone to protect his team went by the roadside now that Lia and James' life forces were linked together.

"You got that right, baby," James said softly while throwing his arm around Lia's waist.

The hospital room's door swung open, and Frank Marshall stepped inside.

"Herrera is still in a coma. They expect he'll make a full recovery. Give or take a day or two."

"Good," Brian remarked. He yanked the release of the recliner's lever, and the chair returned to an upright position. "We need to find out about Sean."

James' hold on Lia tightened.

"He'll be okay," Lia promised.

Josh nodded in agreement with Lia's words. "I don't feel our connection severed—"

Lia's cellphone pinged with numerous incoming notifications. Hoping to hear from her dad, she quickly reached into her sweater's pocket. Bringing the screen up to view, she swiped across the screen. Her eyes quickly read the incoming messages stacked together.

James, tethered to her thoughts, breathed a heavy sigh.

Lia's smile was bright for all to see as she shared the good news.

"My dad says everything is good on his end..."

Lia's smile went a little crooked when she read the other message out loud. "My mother says she is feeling better than ever."

The rest of the room's occupants let out a sigh of relief. Grudgingly, even Frank Marshall showed he was pleased with the outcome.

"She demands I take better precautions in the future, now that she won't be here personally to make sure that I do. She says she will promise severe consequences to anyone failing to provide better protection."

The whole room groaned in unison. Lia took it in stride. After all, their concerns were justified. Now that everyone understood Michelle Robinson didn't make idle threats, it proved just how dangerous the situation could become.

James clamped Lia closer and pressed a quick kiss on her head. His lips formed the words as he stayed pressed to her sweet-smelling hair. "I welcome her worst if I ever fail to keep you safe."

We'll keep each other safe, Lia promised, using her mental connection to him.

Frank Marshall cleared his throat softly and got everyone's attention. "It goes without saying—"

"Yeah, yeah. No talking about what went down at the marina," Josh said, his tone uncertain. He then sighed, his head falling back onto his pillow as he closed his eyes. "Although… do we even know what really went down there?"

"All there is to know," Frank quickly inserted, while his gaze and physical stance implied serious repercussions for anyone who said otherwise, "is that John Robinson died in a laboratory fire years ago. That Herrera and Suarez's men took advantage of a desperate woman, sadly causing her to relapse into a deep psychosis—where it led, unfortunately, to committing crimes against her daughter and law officials under false pretense to save her husband—to whom she thought was alive—from unjust imprisonment and to reunite her family."

"But..." Lia cut in, not liking Frank's harsh description of the sequence of events.

Frank raised his palm, halting her from continuing. "Honey," he spoke softly, shaking his head from side to side, "your mother more than made up for her mistakes when she sacrificed her life to save yours."

The frustration expressed on Lia's face just about broke James' heart. He knew where Frank was going with this and stepped in to lend him some help.

"Lia, sweetheart, Frank is giving us an out here, and we need to take it—for your safety. Whatever is happening with your father—your mother is now protected by her close proximity to him. **You** are not."

"And we need to keep any association to those two far away from you," Frank explained.

Lia sighed, and her shoulders relaxed with understanding. "Because I'm the only emotional link that would have my father returning."

"Exactly," Frank agreed. "So, no one can open up the official file by making any additional inquiries on what went down. But we will need to follow through off the record concerning Herrara. We need to know the full extent of what he knows. I don't want anyone coming for Lia again."

James shot a look toward Josh and then Brian. He turned back and faced Frank Marshall.

"Will we be able to follow through and interview the prisoners?"

"Herrera and Suarez's men, definitely. But the others that showed up last night... are gone."

Josh's mind wandered, and an unwanted thought about the raven-haired beauty popped into his head before sleep claimed him.

James patted Josh's hand before turning to meet Frank's gaze.

"What do you mean... disappeared? To another black-ops division, or gone for good?"

"Gone, as in... escaped. None of those intruders were there when our crew showed up to retrieve them."

Brian let his head fall back against the recliner. His lids blinked several times. Then his gaze went cool, and his expression fell blank. With his attention back on Frank, he said,

"When can we interrogate Herrera's men? We need to find Sean."

The man, named *Sean Patterson*, flickered his eyes open. He found himself in a room bathed in soft light. The windows, covered with sheer fabric curtains, billowed with the slight breeze. Their covering allowed the sunlight to filter in but diffused the harshness of the sun's full rays.

But he couldn't see that far to know the reason for the room's glow.

He raised his hand to hold his head. A throbbing pain hammered throughout his brain in an angry tempo.

"Good, you are awake," said a gentle and calm voice. Footsteps preceded a shape that came to stand beside Sean's bed. He couldn't make out her face. Everything was blurry.

"Everything is fine," the nurse's voice stayed steady, reassuring Sean. She brushed his hand away from his head and rearranged the bandage that his wandering hand had skewed. "You got a nasty bump on the head," she mentioned. Her fingers, now stroking Sean's temples and forehead, provided a soothing touch. "You just need to rest, and the doc says you'll be good as new."

Doc who? His thoughts tried to figure it out.

He blinked rapidly, but nothing became any clearer. The woman's form remained blob-like with that glow of light surrounding her.

It hurt to look up at her. The weights holding his eyelids down–returned. Sean struggled to open them again, needing to know what had happened to him. But it was of no use.

"Hey, before you go back to sleep, how about you give me your name? I'm sure there are people who are looking for you." She touched his arm and shook him gently.

But he didn't answer. For one thing, he was still so tired; words felt like such an effort to form on his lips. Secondly, and more importantly, he didn't say anything because *Sean Patterson didn't know who he was...* His name and everything else remained an empty, blank slate.

As sleep pulled him back under, the woman remained steadfast by his side. Her fingers gently stroked his hand, a constant source of comfort. Her unwavering gaze remained fixed to his face.

"Don't worry about a thing. I'll be here to watch over you," she reassured him.

He placed his trust in her and let his body succumb to the rest he needed, soothed by her presence.

Just as he dropped off to sleep, an insistent thought came through, urging him to prepare as quickly as possible.